"I still feel it's wise that we not spend any more time together than necessary," Kira said. "If you need my help finding someone who can assist you, I'm willing to begin looking tomorrow."

Tarek pushed off the desk and approached her slowly, his intense eyes trained on hers. "You would defy your king's order?"

If he came any closer, she might agree to anything. "I'm sure he would understand if I explained why I can't accommodate you."

His smile was somewhat devious and patently sensual. "You would tell him that we made love on the marble floor in my ballroom?"

That prompted several more images that Kira forced away. "Of course not. I'll simply tell the king my schedule is too full."

He stood in front of her then, a scant few inches between them. "Surely you do not believe he will accept that explanation."

Tarek tucked one side of her chin-length hair behind her ear. "Your eyes fascinate me. The dark blue color is extraordinary, yet it suits your overall beauty."

Here we go again. His charming tactics had sent her straight into trouble the last time, but she couldn't force herself to move away from him. "You can stop the compliments now. You've already had your way with me."

"I wish to have my way with you again."

Dear Reader,

Writing always involves a certain amount of research, but it can be extensive, particularly when the author is featuring a specific location they've never been before. And unless you're lucky enough to schedule a research trip, you're fairly reliant on the internet, which sometimes leads to the syndrome I like to call "Getting Lost on the Web." This happens when you find a link, then follow another link, and another, until you're not quite sure where you began. Once you find your way back around, the trick is to assimilate that information and provide the essence of the place—*essence* being the operative word, unless you're writing a travel book. When it comes to romance, authors are charged with using sensory details, descriptors and characters' reactions to the atmosphere. In other words, we're emotional guides, not tour guides. Challenging, yes. Rewarding, absolutely.

That said, I hope you enjoy your virtual trip to Cyprus, where the majority of this book is set. I also hope you connect with Kira and Tarek as they face life-changing secrets and reluctantly fall in love in this exotic place. But once they return to reality, anything could happen...and everything is possible.

Happy Traveling!

Kristi

THE SHEIKH'S SECRET HEIR

—

KRISTI GOLD

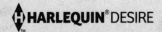

Recycling programs
for this product may
not exist in your area.

ISBN-13: 978-0-373-73393-4

The Sheikh's Secret Heir

Copyright © 2015 by Kristi Goldberg

Printed in U.S.A.

Kristi Gold has a fondness for beaches, baseball and bridal reality shows. She firmly believes that love has remarkable healing powers and feels very fortunate to be able to weave stories of love and commitment. As a bestselling author, a National Readers' Choice Award winner and a Romance Writers of America three-time RITA® Award finalist, Kristi has learned that although accolades are wonderful, the most cherished rewards come from networking with readers. She can be reached through her website at kristigold.com, or through Facebook.

Books by Kristi Gold

HARLEQUIN DESIRE

The Return of the Sheikh
One Night with the Sheikh
From Single Mom to Secret Heiress
The Sheikh's Son
One Hot Desert Night
The Sheikh's Secret Heir

Visit the Author Profile page at Harlequin.com, or kristigold.com, for more titles.

I've said it before, but it bears repeating.
Here's to the happily-ever-after connoisseurs,
the lovers of love stories, the cherished readers
who make our efforts so worthwhile.
You are very much appreciated.

One

As head administrator of the royal palace in the small, autonomous country of Bajul, Kira Darzin had grown accustomed to being summoned on a moment's notice by the king. But as she stood in the study's open doorway, waves of shock washed over her when her gaze came to rest on the undeniably handsome man seated near the desk.

With his neatly trimmed near-black hair, perfectly tailored steel gray suit, and dark Italian loafers, he could have been any successful billionaire. His masculine hands resting casually on the red brocade chair's arms, and the slight lift of his chin, gave him the appearance of an average arrogant autocrat. Yet, when Kira zeroed in on Tarek Azzmar's dark eyes, the power in his intense stare threatened to sweep her away, as it had already done one fateful night not so long ago.

She saw unmistakable confidence. She sensed deep secrets. She felt the pull of provocative danger. A place she had been before both with him, and with another man from her past. A place she vowed to never revisit.

She also noticed that his somewhat regal air made it seem as if he was the one holding court in the private office that belonged to Rafiq Mehdi, the official monarch of Bajul, who was oddly absent. However, Mr. Deeb, the king's personal assistant, stood not far away. When Deeb greeted her, his words sounded tinny to her ears as Tarek rose to his feet, revealing well over six feet of prime male.

With effort, Kira reclaimed enough calm to pretend she had never associated with the Moroccan mogul beyond a few social gatherings. A bald-faced lie. "It's a pleasure to see you again, Mr. Azzmar," she said through a polite and somewhat forced smile.

"The *pleasure* is all mine, Ms. Darzin."

His emphasis on the word unearthed several images in Kira's mind. Hot kisses. Naked bodies. One night of unbelievable passion. And six weeks since that experience, not one word from him.

That sour thought thrust her back to the business at hand. "What might I do for you two gentlemen today?"

Tarek presented the sexy half smile that had melted her resistance like warm chocolate from the first moment they'd met. "Perhaps Mr. Deeb should explain."

The balding, middle-aged assistant stepped forward and pushed his wire-rimmed glasses up on the bridge of his nose. "Actually, I am here representing His Excellency. Both he and Mr. Azzmar request your assistance."

She saw planning an elite soiree in her future. Lovely. "I'm sorry, but I was on my way out for an appointment when I received the message to stop by here. I didn't bring the upcoming schedule with me. If you'll give me a date, I'll begin planning the event immediately."

"This does not involve an event," Tarek said. "It would require your attention for ten days, perhaps even two weeks."

She couldn't imagine any project that would last so long if it didn't involve a special occasion or state dinner. "Do you mind giving me specifics?"

"Mr. Azzmar needs a personal assistant," Deeb began, "and King Mehdi has offered your services until a replacement can be located."

Surely they weren't serious. She glanced at Tarek and, from the all-business expression on his striking face, saw he was quite serious. Regardless, she would not bend to his will and instead, mentally ran through a litany of reasons to decline, minus the most important one—she was too vulnerable when it came to his charisma. "Considering my responsibilities with my position at the palace, I'm afraid that's impossible. Prince Zain, his wife and children will be returning in three days. And next week, Prince Adan's sister-in-law and Sheikh Rayad will be joining them. Someone has to prepare for their arrival."

"We have resolved that issue," Deeb added. "Elena has agreed to assume your responsibilities until you fulfill your duty to Mr. Azzmar."

She had a difficult time believing Elena, former governess and biological mother of the youngest Mehdi prince, Adan, would agree to such a thing. "She hired me as the director of the household so she could retire. It doesn't seem fair to ask this of her."

Deeb scowled. "Our king gave the order and Elena still adheres to his directives."

Kira stifled a retort involving what the king could do with *this* directive. "And I have no say in this matter?"

Before Deeb could respond, Tarek took a step forward to address the royal attaché. "Might I have a word alone with Ms. Darzin?"

Deeb nodded. "Of course. I will return to my office should you require further assistance."

As soon as Deeb left out the door, closing it behind him, Kira turned to Tarek and frowned. "Would you please explain why you didn't reject Rafiq's request in light of what happened between us?"

He leaned back against the desk and folded his arms across his chest. "I made the request, not the king."

Unbelievable. "Why would you want me as your glorified secretary with all the other candidates available among the palace staff?"

"No secretarial work will be involved, and no other candidates intrigue me as you do."

Kira crossed the room to the window, putting much-needed space between them and stared a few seconds at the mountainous terrain before facing him again. "You mean no other candidates have slept with you, correct?"

"I do not recall any measurable sleeping that night."

Neither did Kira, but she did remember one important fact. "True, and then you suddenly disappeared. I assumed you had moved back to Morocco."

"What would the logic be in that since I have recently completed my estate here in Bajul?"

She supposed her hypothesis hadn't made much sense. Then again, neither had letting their relationship go so far during the time when the royal family had been in the States for their cousin Rayad's wedding to Piper Mehdi's sister, Sunny. If she'd only been focused on her job, they wouldn't be having this conversation.

"I just found it odd you haven't been around the past six weeks." And somewhat hurtful, not that she dared admit that to him.

"Actually, I have been traveling abroad."

She almost asked if the *broad* had a name but recognized that word probably wouldn't be a part of his vernacular. "Backpacking in Europe?"

That earned her a confused look. "Completing a multimillion-dollar business venture."

Just what he needed—more money. Kira bit back the snide comment for the time being. "Regardless, I still feel it's wise that we not spend any more time together than necessary, particularly for two weeks. If you need my help finding someone who can assist you, I'm willing to begin looking tomorrow."

He pushed off the desk and approached her slowly, his intense eyes trained on hers. "You would defy your king's order?"

If Tarek came any closer, she might agree to anything. "I'm sure he would understand if I explained why I can't accommodate you."

His smile was somewhat devious and patently sensual. "You would tell him that we made love on the marble floor in my ballroom?"

That prompted several more images that Kira forced away. "Of course not. First of all, we had sex with no love involved. Secondly, no one needs to know that I had an interlude with a palace guest unless I want to lose my job, which I don't. I'll simply tell the king my schedule is too full."

He stood in front of her then, a scant few inches between them. "Surely you do not believe Rafiq Mehdi will accept that explanation."

Not exactly. "All I can do is try. If he rejects my excuse, then I'll think of something else." A spontaneous trip to Canada to visit her parents seemed like a viable explanation.

Tarek moved closer, reached out and tucked one side of her chin-length hair behind her ear. "Your eyes fascinate me. The dark blue color is extraordinary, yet it suits your overall beauty."

Here we go again. His charming tactics had sent her straight into trouble the last time, but she couldn't force herself to move away from him. "You can stop the compliments now. You've already had your way with me."

"I wish to have my way with you again."

His motivation had become all too clear. "Is that what this is all about?"

Fortunately, he dropped his hand, causing her to release the breath she hadn't realized she'd been holding. "No. I sincerely do need an assistant I can trust. You are intelligent and personable and highly regarded by the Mehdis. However, I see no reason not to enjoy each other's company when you come with me to my private seaside escape."

That almost rendered her speechless. Bajul was located in the mountains, not a sea in sight. "You plan to take me out of the country?"

"Yes. Cyprus, where I am preparing to launch my latest venture, an exclusive resort. That is why I require your assistance."

Kira couldn't ignore visions of beautiful beaches, romantic sunsets and midnight swims. She also couldn't quell her suspicions. "What exactly would my role be?"

"I would like you to approve the final decisions on the resort's kitchen layout, as well as the interior design. You could also advise the hotel manager on hiring staff."

"My forte isn't interior design." Even if it was somewhat of a passion.

"Are you not overseeing the palace restoration that will begin in a few months? And do you not plan every palace event, including the food and décor?"

Clearly he knew all about her upcoming assignments. Too bad she couldn't say the same about his motives. "Yes, but—"

He pressed a fingertip against her lips. "Please know I will not force you to come with me. If you decide you cannot tolerate my presence for a mere two weeks, then I will seek other avenues. I do request you give my offer some thought."

She'd do nothing but think about it from this point

forward. And then she would tell him no. "When do you need my answer?"

"By tomorrow morning. My plane will be ready to depart in the afternoon."

With her thoughts spinning round like a carousel, Kira checked her watch. "Fine. I'll let you know as soon as possible. Right now I have somewhere I need to be."

His features turned stern. "Do you have a new paramour?"

"Doctor's appointment." As if *that* was any of his business.

Now he appeared concerned. "Are you not feeling well?"

Fatigued and edgy, but well enough to function. "Just a follow-up visit for a slight case of the flu I had a week ago," she said as she brushed past him and headed to the door. But before she could leave, Tarek called her name in a deep, chill-inducing voice.

She sighed and turned toward him again. "What?"

"Perhaps you need relaxation to recover from this flu. Cyprus is the premier place to do that very thing."

"You wouldn't worry I might expose you?"

He hinted at a smile. "You have already exposed me and I thoroughly enjoyed the experience."

That deserved an eye roll, which she gave him. "You're not helping your cause, Tarek. I won't agree even to consider accompanying you unless you promise to halt the innuendo and the thinly veiled seduction."

He tried on an innocent look, but it failed to impress her. "I can only promise that I will try. I do promise to make the journey worth your while."

His methods of making that happen concerned her most of all. "I'll keep that in mind. At the moment, I have to go."

He ate up the space between them in a matter of seconds, took her hand and kissed it. "Until we meet again."

Don't hold your breath, she thought as she hurried into the hallway. Wisdom dictated she refuse to go with him anywhere, especially to an exotic locale where she could forget her worries, and most likely would forget herself.

She needed to remember he was exactly the kind of man she'd strived to shun. And after tomorrow morning, when she'd tell him he could find someone else to do his bidding, she would have absolutely no reason to speak to him again.

"You're pregnant."

Balanced on the edge of the uncomfortable exam table, Kira tugged on her skirt hem and stared blankly at Dr. Maysa Mehdi, presiding queen of Bajul and resident village physician. "Excuse me?" she asked, her voice barely a croak.

Maysa scooted the rolling stool closer and flipped her lengthy dark braid back over one shoulder. "When I ordered your lab work last week, I had them add a pregnancy test, in light of your symptoms. That test was positive and all the rest were normal."

Kira pinched the bridge of her nose and closed her eyes against the sudden headache. "This can't be happening."

"I'm afraid it is, and it appears you are not pleased with the news."

Kira opened her eyes and exhaled slowly. "I'm shocked. First of all, I've been on the pill for years. Secondly, I've been exposed only one time in several years." And some exposure it had been.

Maysa opened the chart resting in her lap and scanned the text. "I notice here you have not requested a refill on your birth control in two months."

Guilty. "I suppose I've been so busy I basically forgot. And I had no real need for them." Until Tarek Azzmar slipped into her life like a thief of hearts and destroyed her self-imposed celibacy.

"Perhaps you were so busy that you forgot to take your pills prior to the time of your lovemaking?" Maysa asked.

Guilty again. "Yes, but only for two, maybe three days tops."

"That is all it takes, Kira."

She suddenly felt like an absolute fool. An unequivocal idiot. "Believe me, I never planned to be with this man."

Maysa smiled. "At times, plans go awry and mistakes are made. How will this man feel about the pregnancy?"

She had no clue how Tarek would react, or if she would even tell him. "I truly don't know. In reality, I barely know him beyond a few social functions. It was something neither of us expected to happen."

"If he is a man of honor," Maysa began, "he will accept the responsibility of raising a child."

If only she could claim he was a man of honor, but all signs pointed to the contrary. "I suppose only time will tell."

Maysa closed the chart and came to her feet. "I suppose you will learn soon enough. In the meantime, you'll need to take better care of yourself, including getting more rest."

As much as Kira had always dreamed of having a child, reaching that goal now hadn't figured into her immediate plans, especially when considering her duties at the palace. "I have no idea how to balance work and this pregnancy. And I can't imagine what my parents will say when I tell them."

Maysa frowned. "They would not welcome a grand-child?"

"Since my mother's Canadian and open-minded, she would be fine with it. My father, on the other hand, is from Bajul and quite the traditionalist. He would not be pleased to know his unwed daughter is giving birth."

Maysa rested a hand on Kira's shoulder. "If you de-termine the timing is not right for you, perhaps you should consider adoption."

Since she was an adopted child, a fact few people knew, she had mixed feelings about that option. "I don't know if I could hand over my baby to strangers."

"Some believe that is the most unselfish thing a woman can do for her child, myself included. Regard-less, you do not need to decide immediately. I am going to prescribe prenatal vitamins that you should begin taking."

When Maysa turned to the counter and began scribbling on a prescription pad, Kira slid off the table and pressed her palm against the small of her aching back. At least now she knew why she'd been so tired and slightly nauseated. At least now she could explain the absence of her period. At least now she could formulate a plan for the future and decide if it would include the father of her baby.

It suddenly occurred to her that perhaps she should reconsider Tarek's offer. Not only would she get some rest, but two weeks might be enough time to determine if he wanted children, and hopefully whether he would be father material. If neither applied, she could decide where she would go from there.

As soon as she returned to the palace, she would seek out Tarek Azzmar and ask a few more questions about his proposition. Only then could she establish if spending more time with him would be worth the risk.

"Miss Darzin is here to see you, sir."

Tarek glanced up to find the young woman he'd recently hired standing in the doorway to his private study. He hesitated, surprised by the announcement. "Send her in, Adara."

After the servant disappeared, Tarek set the quarterly reports on the teakwood end table, rose from the club chair and waited for what seemed an interminable amount of time before Kira appeared, looking as beautiful as the first time he'd noticed her across a crowded reception hall.

After tugging at the hem of her blue blazer, she swept one hand through her chin-length golden-brown hair and surveyed the room. "It's nice to see you've completed all the décor."

"It is very nice to see you."

"Thank you," she said with cool formality. "Everything looks extremely different from the last time I visited."

The visit Tarek had not forgotten. The tour of the newly built, empty mansion had ended with a passionate encounter on the floor of the grand ballroom. "I still have some work to do on the third floor suites. How was your appointment with the physician, if you do not mind my asking?"

"I received a clean bill of health." She then strolled into the room and breezed past him to study the volumes of books on the shelves behind his desk. "You have very eclectic tastes when it comes to novels. I had no idea you were so interested in true crime."

He slid his hands into his pockets and approached her slowly. "Did you come here to approve my reading material?"

Finally, she faced him. "Actually, I came here to discuss the trip to Cyprus. I have a few more questions before I make my decision."

His optimism rose when he thought she might have reconsidered his proposition. "What would you wish to know?"

"You're certain we would be gone only two weeks?"

"Unless unforeseen issues arise. Granted, you would be required to stay only that length of time. Should you decide to depart earlier, I agree to accommodate your request."

She folded her arms beneath her breasts and attempted a smile. "Then you don't plan to hold me hostage against my will?"

Her assumption angered him somewhat. "I would never hold a woman captive." At least not in the literal sense.

"That's somewhat reassuring."

"Do you have more questions?"

"Yes. I still have concerns about your motives."

He could not fault her for those concerns. "Are you worried that I will attempt to seduce you? Perhaps persuade you to make love with me on my private beach, in my private pool or in my rather large steam shower?"

She pointed a finger at him. "That's exactly what concerns me most."

He opted to feign ignorance. "As it was when we made love the first time—"

"The *only* time we had sex," she interjected.

He hoped to change that soon, yet he would use gentle persuasion, not coercion. "As I was saying, I would never force you to do what you do not wish to do. And I assure you, my motives involve business, not necessarily pleasure, although I am not averse to that."

"You've made that quite clear, and that worries me," she said as she brushed past him and claimed the chair he had recently vacated.

Following her lead, he dropped onto the leather sofa across from her. His eyes followed the movement of her hand as she ran her palm down her thigh to smooth her skirt. He immediately imagined that hand on his body and then, with effort, forced the fantasy away. "Rest assured, if you join me, I will maintain my distance if that is what you desire."

"That's what I desire," she stated, yet her faltering gaze led Tarek to believe she was not at all certain.

"I will respect your wishes." Unless their incontrovertible chemistry dictated otherwise.

She appeared unconvinced. "Tarek, you're a brilliant businessman, but you're still a man. You possess two brains and if the situation arises, so will your secondary brain. You would have to maintain a great deal of control."

He would not attempt to debate her on that point. "You will have your own quarters at your disposal and you will have to endure my presence only during our business dealings."

She began to twirl the silver band on her right ring finger. "Look, I enjoy your company and I have since we first met. I'm just not in the market to enjoy it too much again."

Feeling satisfied over the admission, he inclined his head and studied her. "Then you did enjoy our encounter?"

She hesitated a few seconds. "I suppose I have to admit that I did, with the exception of the marble floor."

"That is why I allowed you to be on top."

"After you had me on my back."

"On your back so that I could quickly remove your clothes and run my mouth down your body to facilitate your—"

"We don't need to go there."

He could not suppress a grin. "Ah, but I already have,

and considering the sounds you made, I do not believe you were disappointed."

She quickly stood and sighed. "I'm not in the mood to take a journey down memory lane, so I'm going to return to the palace now."

Tarek came to his feet. "Shall I expect you on the plane tomorrow?"

When she did not immediately respond, he held his breath and hoped. "I'll let you know tonight, when you're dining at the palace."

He frowned. "I did not realize you were aware of the invitation."

She sent him a disparaging look before crossing the room. "It's my job to know everything about the royal family and their esteemed guests," she said on her way out.

After she disappeared, Tarek checked his watch, reclaimed his chair and picked up the phone to make his daily call to the other female in his life. If he did not do it soon, he would regret the oversight. A few moments passed before he was greeted with the familiar, quiet, *"Ahlan?"*

He opted to answer in English, not Arabic, to test her acumen, as he had since teaching her the language. "Did you receive my gift, Yasmin?"

"I did!" she said with the marked exuberance of a typical five-year-old. "He is lovely."

That was not how he would describe the street-roving mutt. "I am glad you are pleased. Will you take good care of him?"

"Yes, I will. I promise to feed him and give him

water and take him for walks. What shall we name him?"

"That is entirely up to you, Yasmin."

"I will have to think about it. When are you coming home? Soon, I hope."

No matter what said he told her, he would disappoint her. "I told you about the new resort before I left Morocco. I still have much work to do on it."

"You are always working. I wish you would take me with you."

That would be impossible at this point in time. Very few knew of her existence, and he wanted to keep it that way. "Perhaps someday. In the meantime, take care."

"I will."

"I shall see you in a month when I return."

A span of silence passed before she said, "I miss you."

"I miss you as well, Yasmin." And he certainly did, though too much affection would serve neither of them.

As soon as he hung up the phone, Tarek began to contemplate his previous conversation with Kira and her erroneous assumptions.

It's my job to know everything about the royal family and their esteemed guests...

Little did Kira know, she was not privy to most aspects of his private life, as it had been with all friends and former lovers. Not only in regard to the child, but she was also unaware that he retained an important piece of the Mehdi puzzle. Only he held the key and no one else, not even the current monarch and his brothers. He harbored a great secret that might have died along with his parents, save an old man's conscience and overwhelming guilt.

Since gaining that knowledge, he had been bound by a pledge to keep the information guarded out of respect for his mother, yet he had grown weary of the pretense. He wanted answers. He demanded answers. He vowed to do whatever he must to gain that information, and he hoped Kira Darzin could aid him in his search.

From the minute he'd met her, he had sensed she would know much about the Mehdis, and he would continue to gain her trust in an effort to convince her to confide in him. That had been his primary goal in the beginning, until he had crossed the boundaries into ill-advised desire. He had not intended to be as preoccupied by her and he would do well not to let his base urges rule his rationality.

If his plan with Kira did not succeed, he would continue to covertly search for confirmation through every means possible, work his way into the royal sons' good graces, then he would properly introduce himself as the bastard son of the former king of Bajul.

Their brother.

Two

Every evening at six o'clock sharp, Kira prepared to deliver her usual courtesy call. It was incumbent that she made certain all needs were met, though tonight that wouldn't be easy, considering she would have to face the father of her child. After she walked into the elaborate dining room, she found the lengthy mahogany table populated with the usual royal residents—King Rafiq and his wife, Maysa, along with the newlyweds, Adan and Piper—and one not-so-usual sophisticated man dressed in a beige silk suit, sitting to the right of Rafiq. Anyone who didn't know the Mehdis might mistake Tarek Azzmar as a relative, when in reality his only ties to the royals were big business, Middle Eastern roots and an abundance of good looks.

When Tarek leveled his gaze on her, Kira's thoughts

spun away like a desert whirlwind. She sincerely wanted to look away, yet it was as if he had her completely under some macabre magical spell. "Magical" would definitely describe his thorough kisses, his very skilled hands, his expertise at lovemaking, his obvious virility....

"Is there another bun in the oven, Kira?"

Taken aback by Adan Mehdi's query, Kira directed her attention to the youngest prince, her face splashed with heat. "Excuse me?"

He held up the empty basket. "We are out of bread."

Apparently, she was plagued by secret pregnancy paranoia. "I'll see to that immediately."

"And, Kira, if it's not too much trouble, I'd like more water, please," Adan's auburn-haired wife added as she leaned back in the chair, providing a peek at her rounded belly. "I'm so thirsty I think I'm giving birth to a trout, not a mammal."

Kira experienced a brief bout of envy when Adan and Piper exchanged a loving look. At least they had each other. At least Piper wouldn't be raising her baby alone.

Whether that would be the case for Kira when it came to her own child still remained to be seen. "I'll be certain to have the server deliver you an entire pitcher of water, as she should have done at the beginning of the meal. She's new and still trying to gain her bearings. I also believe she's a bit starstruck over her introduction to royalty."

Piper's grin expanded as she waved a hand toward Tarek. "I think she's quite taken with our guest."

Kira ventured a glance and discovered Tarek didn't seem at all disturbed by the conjecture. When he failed to reply, she focused on the eldest Mehdi son. "Is the dinner tonight to your liking, Your Majesty?"

"As usual, the fare is excellent," Rafiq replied as he regarded Tarek. "Would you would like more of the chicken kabobs, Mr. Azzmar?"

Tarek pushed his empty plate aside and leveled his gaze on Kira. "Not presently, but it was delicious. I particularly enjoyed the garlic yogurt sauce. Please give my compliments to the chef."

Adan presented his usual dimpled smile. "Perhaps you would like to deliver the message yourself and inspect the help further, Tarek."

Piper elbowed her husband, causing him to wince. "Stop it, Adan. I'm sure Tarek is more than capable of finding a date."

Adan grimaced. "Bloody hell, wife. I like it much better when your pregnancy hormones lead to pleasure and not pain. I was simply suggesting Tarek might be interested in keeping company with a woman who is obviously smitten with him."

"Your bride is correct," Tarek added. "I am very selective when it comes to female companionship. Although the server is attractive, she is much too young, therefore she does not hold my interest."

After the billionaire nailed her with another pointed look, Kira snatched the basket from the table and began backing toward the door. "I'll let the chef know you're all pleased with the meal and I'll send someone out with more bread and water. Good evening."

With that, she spun around and strode into the nearby kitchen, muttering a few mild oaths at herself over her inability to ignore Tarek. She mumbled a few more aimed at the businessman who seemed bent on keeping her off balance.

"Please take more rolls and water to the table immediately," she said to the recently hired, very pretty fresh-faced staff member. "And from this point forward, pay more attention to the family and guests' needs. Prince Adan requires more bread than most, and always make certain there is a pitcher of water close at hand in the dining room."

The young woman quickly took the basket, filled it with rolls, grabbed a water pitcher and scurried away, her brown ponytail bouncing in time with her gait. Kira then leaned back against the steel prep table while the chef remained at the stove, where Kira's own mother had once stood, preparing the finishing touches on dessert as several of the staff members engaged in clean-up. She rubbed both temples with her fingertips and closed her eyes against the beginnings of another nagging headache. The reason for that headache happened to be seated in the dining room, acting as if he practically owned the palace.

One arrogant man. One gorgeous egomaniac. One weakness she couldn't afford to have.

"Might I have a few moments alone with you, Miss Darzin?"

Speaking of the sexy devil himself. Kira's eyes snapped open at the deep timbre of his now-familiar voice. "Actually, I'm rather busy at the moment, Mr. Azzmar."

Tarek strolled into the kitchen as if he were king of the castle, hands planted in his pockets. "Then I would be happy to speak with you about our plans while you continue your duties."

Conversing with him in front of the staff could be detrimental on several levels. She could only imagine what they were already thinking. "I suppose we can discuss your needs in the corridor." And that sounded entirely too suggestive. "*Needs* as in your need for an administrative assistant."

"Ah, yes, that need." He swept a hand toward the opening to the hallway. "After you."

Kira rushed out of the room, unable to avoid the curious glances of the employees. She continued down the passage with the current thorn in her side trailing behind her and pushed out the doors leading to the courtyard. Once there, she turned and practically face-planted into Tarek's broad chest. "Do you mind giving me some space?"

He took a step back. "Is this better?"

Better would entail having the persistent man standing several yards away, not less than a foot in front of her. "As long as you don't come any closer, that will do."

His expression turned somber. "Do you fear me, Kira?"

"Of course not." Not in a traditional sense, yet she did fear the way he made her feel—vulnerable.

"Do you believe I would never do anything to harm you?"

"Yes, I believe that." He wouldn't, at least not physically, but he had dealt her an unsolicited emotional blow six weeks ago.

He released a rough sigh. "Then I must admit I am somewhat confused by your recent attitude. When we first met, I had several opportunities to attempt to seduce you, yet I did not. Instead, we spent many hours engaged in casual conversation, and only conversation, until the night we spent together. I assumed we had established a measure of trust between us."

"I thought so, too, until that night."

"Clearly I have been mistaken in my belief that our pursuit of pleasure was mutual."

"It was mutual," she stated firmly. "We were both consenting adults."

"Then why are treating me as if I am a pariah not worthy of your regard?"

He didn't understand, and Kira wasn't certain she could explain. Still, she had to try, and that entailed revealing how his careless *disregard* had made her feel. "That isn't my intent. What we shared was a mistake, not only because I crossed a line I shouldn't have crossed with a palace guest, but because you're clearly not the type of man to maintain a monogamous lifestyle. That became apparent when I didn't hear a word from you after that night, as if you'd had your way with me and tossed me aside."

A hint of anger flashed in his eyes. "You are making an erroneous assumption, Kira. As I have told you, I was seeing to business. I do not treat women as chattel."

"They why did you fail to inform me you would be leaving?"

"I was only honoring your request not to approach you again."

He definitely had her there. "True, but I didn't mean we should completely sever all ties. Your actions made me feel used."

He streaked a hand over his jaw and his gaze momentarily drifted away before he returned it to her. "My sincerest apologies, and I am sorry that you have so little faith that you would believe I considered our interlude as nothing more than a diversion. If you wish me to lie and say that I do not want you now, I cannot do that. I cannot promise that if you decide to join me, I will be able to discard my desire for you. If you have trouble accepting this, perhaps you should decline accompanying me to Cyprus. I prefer you not do that, but I will leave the decision to you."

As he turned to leave, Kira realized that if she rejected his request, she would be giving up the opportunity to know him better. To learn if he might be the kind of man who would be open to raising a child. She couldn't squander that opportunity for both her and their baby's sake. "Tarek, wait. We need to talk."

He faced her again and sent her a frustrated look. "I have said all that I have to say about this matter."

"But I haven't," she said as she strode to him. "I'm sorry that I've jumped to conclusions, and I do realize you were only following my instructions. If we can get past this, I would really like to start over and return to our original relationship."

"Which was?"

"Friendship." When he scowled, she added, "Unless you're not able to maintain a friendship with a woman."

"I would find it difficult to go back after what we shared, but I would be willing to try."

"And if that's true, then I'd be willing to go with you to Cyprus."

"You will?" Both his expression and tone reflected disbelief.

"Yes. We could spend the time together getting to know each other better."

Now he looked skeptical. "I am a very private person when it comes to certain aspects of my life."

"I'm not suggesting you show me a financial statement and I don't expect to rifle through your underwear drawer for secrets."

His expression turned hard, unforgiving. "Why would you believe I have secrets?"

His reaction took Kira aback and led her to believe he might be withholding something. But so was she. "Everyone has secrets, Tarek. I have no reason to ask you to reveal yours to me, unless you're doing something illegal."

He seemed to relax somewhat. "I assure you that all my business dealings are aboveboard and within the law."

"That is good to know." Now for the question that would seal her fate for the next two weeks, depending on his response. "Since I've laid out my terms, does the offer to join you still stand?"

"Yes. My driver will come for you at 4:00 p.m. and escort you safely to the airport."

She had less than twenty-four hours to prepare. Twenty-two hours, to be exact, to change her mind. But, with so much riding on this trip, she had to follow through. "I suppose I will see you tomorrow afternoon then."

"I am looking forward to it. Sleep well, Kira."

"You too, Tarek."

As neither of them made a move to depart, a tension as thick as smoky mountain haze hung between them. The craving to kiss Tarek settled over Kira, and to counteract that desire, she started toward the door to his back, intent on a quick escape. Yet as she brushed past him, Tarek clasped her wrist, halting her progress. "If I establish nothing else during our time together, Kira," he began, "I am determined to win your trust again."

Kira responded with a shaky smile and, after he released her, left him standing alone in the courtyard.

Trust between them was a slippery slope, for if Tarek Azzmar eventually learned what she'd been withholding from him, he would probably never trust her again.

She couldn't worry about that now. First, she had to finish her duties for the night and pack for the trip. Hopefully she wouldn't be disturbed.

"Are you busy, *cara*?"

Sequestered in her quaint but comfortable live-in quarters, Kira looked up from the suitcase to find sixty-something, Italian-born Elena Battelli hovering inside the bedroom doorway sporting her neatly coiffed silver hairdo, standard palace-issued navy suit and trademark kind smile. "I always have time for you, Elena. Come in."

"Good. This will take only a few minutes."

After placing the last of her clothing into the bag, Kira zipped it closed, lifted it from the cream-colored bench and set it on the floor at her feet. "All done. Did I forget something when we met earlier today to go over the schedules?"

"You covered everything in regard to business, but I do have an important question."

"And that is?"

Elena strolled into the room and roosted on the edge of the bed. "How well do you know this Tarek Azzmar?"

That she hadn't expected. Time to bring out a half-truth. "I've met him a few times during social gatherings. Why?"

"Several rumors have been circulating among the staff that perhaps you and Mr. Azzmar are...how do I say this? Lovers?"

If it were truly possible to swallow one's tongue, Kira would have accomplished that feat following the verbal bombshell. "You know how people talk, Elena," she said once she'd recovered her ability to speak. "Gossip is as common as morning coffee in this place. You can't believe everything you hear."

"Then why are you blushing, *cara*?"

Her hands automatically went to her flushed face before she quickly dropped them to her sides. "It's embarrassing to think you're the butt of false hearsay."

"Then you and Mr. Azzmar are not romantically involved?"

"No, we're not." At least not anymore.

"Then he is not the father of your unborn child?"

Kira collapsed onto the bench from absolute shock. Did she already look pregnant? Had Maysa breached doctor-patient privilege and mentioned it to Elena? Both theories were utterly preposterous. "I have no idea where you would get the idea I'm pregnant."

After reaching into her blazer pocket, Elena withdrew a large white plastic bottle. "These fell out of your bag when you hurried out of the office following our meeting."

Kira remained frozen on the spot as she eyed the prenatal vitamins. She chastised herself for being so careless, or perhaps she'd subconsciously wanted Elena to find out. Consciously, she thought, for the time being, it was best to rack her brain for some plausible explanation that didn't involve the truth. "I've heard they're good for your hair and nails."

Elena presented a cynical smile. "I know several good herbal supplements that would suffice without expense. I also know when a young woman is concealing the truth from a presumed naïve senior citizen."

She should have known better than to attempt to pull the wool over the eyes of the wisest person she'd ever known. Resigned to the fact she couldn't wriggle out of this, and tired of denying a truth that should be bringing her joy, Kira collapsed onto the bench and sighed. "All right. I am pregnant. But I can't risk everyone knowing before I tell the baby's father." And her poor, clueless parents.

Elena pushed off the bed, claimed the spot beside Kira, and took her hand. "You are under no obligation to reveal the identity of the man who knocked you up."

Hearing "knocked up" coming from the woman's mouth sent Kira into a fit of laughter. Once she recovered, unwelcome and unexpected tears began to flow. They only increased when Elena handed her a handkerchief and patted her arm. "I don't know what to do, Elena. I'm so afraid of how Tarek is going to react to this news." A moment passed before awareness dawned that she'd let the truth tiger out of the cage. "And I'm sorry I lied to you about him in the beginning."

"That is understandable, *cara*," Elena replied, sincere sympathy in her tone. "This is not something that should be broadcast throughout the palace before you have spoken with the appropriate parties. You do plan to tell him while you're away together, don't you?"

She swiped the moisture from her cheeks. "I'm not sure I'm going to tell him at all. I agreed to this trip in part to find out more about him, and hopefully to gauge how he would react to the news. Maybe even to discover if he's fit to be a father to my child."

"Then you are planning to keep the baby?"

She couldn't think much past the upcoming two weeks and deciding whether to inform Tarek. "Maysa and I briefly discussed adoption, but I don't know if I could let my baby go. Does that make me selfish?"

"No, *cara mia*. That makes you a mother."

When Elena went silent, stared off into space and

smiled, Kira's curiosity overcame her. "What are you thinking about?"

"The day your parents brought you back to Bajul after their return from a lengthy trip to Canada. Most people assumed Chandra had hidden her pregnancy from everyone, but I suspected you were a precious gift they had received while they were away. Your mother confided in me not long after."

One more stunning revelation in a long line of many within the palace's hallowed halls. "You knew about my adoption?"

"Yes, I did, and I have kept the secret since your birth. You can trust me with yours as well."

She knew Elena's word was good as gold, but she wondered what other secrets the woman might be privy to. "Do you know anything about my birth parents other than they were very young? Mother and Father would never talk about them when I asked, and when I tried to contact my biological mother, she wasn't willing to speak with me."

Elena shook her head. "I am sorry I do not. I am also sorry they have not been forthcoming with that information, though I do understand their reasoning on some level. My son can attest to that. Adan spent his life believing another woman to be his mother."

Kira wrapped an arm around her shoulder and gave her a gentle squeeze. "You had no choice in the matter, Elena. From what you've said, you were following King Aadil's orders to keep Adan's true parentage concealed. At least the two of you now have the opportunity to know each other as mother and son."

"Yet we cannot live openly that way," Elena said. "Very few people know the truth, as it should be. Rafiq cannot afford another scandal after barely surviving his marriage to a divorcée with his authority intact."

And she could very well hand them another huge scandal if anyone learned that Tarek had fathered her child. Perhaps she should resign and move to Canada. No. She could not live off her parents' good graces, especially when her papa would be so disapproving of her unwed-mother status. But what other options did she have?

She was simply too tired to plan so far ahead. That fatigue filtered out as she hid a yawn behind her hand.

Elena got to her feet and patted Kira's cheek. "You need to sleep, *cara mia*. When I was expecting Adan, I remember nodding off in midsentence."

Kira rose and drew her into a quick embrace. "Thank you for listening to me. I'm honestly relieved that I have someone I can trust to talk to about this."

"You can always trust me, dear one. And should you need my counsel following your journey, I will be here."

"Thank you."

Elena then started toward the door, only to face Kira once more. "Since you obviously have decided to raise your child, I truly hope you find Tarek Azzmar to be an honorable man and a worthy father. As you have learned, every child deserves to know their legacy if at all possible."

With that, she walked out of the bedroom, leaving Kira to ponder her words as she readied for bed. Her instincts told her to trust in Tarek. Her past dictated she be overly cautious. Falling victim to a man with dishonorable intentions had taught her that hard lesson eight years ago. She sincerely hoped that the father of her baby proved to be the man she had at first believed him to be, and not someone who judged a woman for her lack of good breeding, led her on, then left her heart in tatters.

Only time would tell if the real Tarek Azzmar turned out to be a huge disappointment, or a pleasant surprise.

Three

He was pleasantly surprised when she entered the plane, yet disappointed at her obvious aloofness when she muttered a greeting. She wore a somewhat sheer blue blouse and fitted white skirt rising a few inches above her knee, and that alone had him battling the urge to invite her into the onboard sleeping quarters, a request she would no doubt reject. He had to respect her friendship request for the time being, yet he could not be certain how long that would last.

Despite that, Tarek sent Kira a guarded smile as he showed her to the black leather seat and claimed the one set against the bulkhead opposite hers. They remained silent during takeoff, the lack of communication continuing as the pilot permitted them to move about the cabin.

As Tarek unbuckled his seat belt, Kira removed a magazine from the bag resting at her feet. "Would you like something to drink?" he asked as he stood.

"I'm fine, thank you," she said as she surveyed the area. "This is a very nice plane, maybe even a bit nicer than the Mehdis', although smaller. With all this black and white, it reminds me of a four-star boutique with wings. I'm surprised you don't have an onboard bartender."

"Due to the short duration of the flight, no attendants are necessary."

"Three hours isn't exactly short."

"It is not long enough to justify bringing along a full staff." In truth, he wanted privacy more than he had wanted someone waiting on him. "Therefore I will serve as your host. My wish is your command."

"Again, I have no wishes, but your hospitality is appreciated."

Frustrated, Tarek moved to the onboard bar, reached into the upper cabinet above the refrigerator and retrieved a bottle of wine that he had reserved for a special occasion. Apparently Kira did not see anything special about traveling with him. At the moment, he needed something to cut through the tension, even if it came from a glass of twenty-thousand-dollar French premier cru.

Once he returned to his seat, he found her flipping through random pages. "What are you reading?"

She paused and lifted the magazine from her lap, then set it back down. "Just something to pass the time."

"I have never had an affinity for tabloids."

That had earned him Kira's undivided attention and a scornful look. "It's not a tabloid. It features book and movie reviews and human interest stories."

"If one is interested in reading about adultery, illegal drug use and secret pregnancies involving Hollywood stars. Of course, the secret is soon revealed when paparazzi capture photos of the expectant actresses on the beach and release them to the general public. The concept sickens me."

She raised a thin brow. "The photos or the pregnant starlets?"

"Both, in a sense. It seems it is a rite of passage among the rich and famous to populate the world, with or without the benefit of matrimony."

"Now I understand. You're a traditionalist when it comes to marriage before the baby carriage."

She did not truly understand at all, nor would she without knowing his goal. "I am a pragmatist. It is immaterial to me whether someone marries or not before giving birth. I strongly believe that one should consider the atmosphere into which they are bringing a child. In my opinion, thrusting someone so young into the spotlight could be detrimental to their well-being."

Her gaze drifted away momentarily before she tossed the magazine back in the bag. "I suppose since everyone knows your business when you're in the spotlight, that's definitely a risk."

He took a drink of the wine and set it into the holder built into the seat's arm. "I would not wish to be placed under a microscope on a daily basis."

"But you have no problem having your face splashed

across financial publications. And yes, I've seen a few of those covers featuring your smiling face."

He briefly wondered if perhaps someone in the royal family had known of his existence prior to their introduction. "Where did you come by this knowledge?"

"The internet. I did some research before you visited the palace the first time."

"An order from the king?"

"No. I took the initiative on my own. I make a point to learn about guests of the royal family."

He relaxed somewhat. "What else do you know about my life?"

She shrugged. "Not all that much, other than you're in the top fifteen on the list of the wealthiest men in the world."

"Top ten."

"Forgive me for my ignorance. I also know that you are somewhat of a philanthropist. I read an article where you opened an orphanage in Mexico City a while back."

A pet project he had felt compelled to complete for personal reasons. "There was a need, and I had the means to fulfill that need."

"I'm sure the tax write-off doesn't hurt."

He bristled at her continual questioning of his motives. "I have global holdings in several countries with varying tax structures. I assure you that compassion, not company write-offs, drives my charitable efforts."

"I'm sorry," she said, sounding somewhat contrite. "I tend to be wary of men with an overabundance of money."

"Why is that?"

"Personal reasons."

He suspected he knew what those reasons might be. "Who was he?"

"I don't understand what you're asking."

The way she shifted in her seat and looked away indicated she chose to be evasive, confirming his conjecture. "Who was the wealthy man who broke your heart?"

"What makes you think this has anything to do with a man?"

"I can sense these things."

She sighed, then hid a yawn behind her hand. "Yes, my attitude stems from a former relationship. Actually, he was my fiancé. And if it's all the same to you, I'd rather not discuss it. I didn't sleep well last night and I'd like to take a nap."

He vowed to revisit the topic at a later time. "We have still have hours before we arrive in Cyprus. That should give you ample time to rest. You will find the sleeping quarters at the rear of the plane."

"I really don't need a bed to take a nap. I'll be fine right here."

He could think of more favorable ways to use the onboard bed. "If you are concerned that I might attempt to join you, put your mind at ease. I do not require any sleep."

"I highly doubt you'd want to join me to sleep."

He returned her unexpected smile. "You know me well."

"Not as well as I hope to know you before the end of this trip."

Though he found her comment somewhat curious, he decided not to assume too much. "If you're determined to refuse the offer of my bed, push the button on the right arm to release the footrest. The one to your left will recline the back."

After complying, Kira stretched out, turned on her side and closed her eyes. "Wake me up in thirty minutes."

Tarek finished off the wine and poured another glass as an afterthought. Rarely did he imbibe aside from the occasional social setting due to his need to remain in absolute control. Yet as he returned to his seat, he acknowledged the woman before him was as intoxicating as a shot of straight Russian vodka. In sleep, she looked innocent, yet he had experienced anything but innocence during their interlude. She had been a willing lover, exciting and experimental. Remembering those blissful moments now prompted a building pressure in his groin, causing him to bring his attention back to Kira.

With her upturned nose and the delicate line of her jaw, he saw little that indicated she would hail from Bajul, aside from the slightly golden color of her skin. Evidently her mother's Canadian roots had taken genetic precedence over her father's Middle Eastern heritage. Regardless, her beauty could not be denied and he had given up on doing that very thing.

During this adventure, he did hope to find out more about her, including the details of the miscreant who had emotionally destroyed her and filled her with distrust. More important, he needed to prove he was not the kind of man to fill a woman with false promises. Eventually he might take a wife and settle down, but not until he achieved his ultimate goal of building more wealth and power. Enough wealth and power to match the Mehdis. What better way to exact revenge for his denied birthright?

Kira awoke long enough to depart the plane that had been secured in a private hangar, only to enter an extravagant black limousine and drift off once again en route to Tarek's Cyprus home. She came back into consciousness a while later, mortified to discover her cheek resting on his shoulder. Had she snored? Drooled? Hopefully none of the above.

After straightening and scooting over, Kira adjusted the hem of her white pencil skirt, which had climbed up her thighs to a point that bordered on indecency. "I'm sorry," she muttered as the car navigated the drive. "I guess I needed more sleep than I realized."

"No apology necessary," he replied as the limo came to a stop. "I enjoyed having you so close. Granted, I was somewhat concerned that I might have to carry you into the house, although that would not have been a great burden."

Maybe not a burden for him, but a total embarrassment for her. "I'll endeavor to stay awake for the remainder of the evening."

When the driver opened the door, Kira realized the sun had already begun to set, yet enough light existed to witness the grandeur of the white, expansive estate with manicured tropical gardens and a four-car garage.

She accepted Tarek's offered hand as he helped her out of the car and followed him silently up the stone path. A man dressed in a white suit greeted them on the front porch, then opened the heavy wooden double doors wide. "Welcome back, Mr. Azzmar."

"It is good to be back, Alexios," he replied. "Please see to it that Ms. Darzin's luggage is delivered to her quarters immediately."

"As you wish, sir," the man said with a nod before making his way to the car.

Tarek turned to Kira and gestured toward the open doors. "After you."

When Kira stepped inside the foyer, she was taken aback by the ultramodern décor that directly contrasted with Tarek's newly built traditional mansion in Bajul. White and steel-gray leather sofas and chairs, accented with black and turquoise pillows, were set about the massive living room, accompanied by several tables comprised of glass and chrome. An enormous curved television hung above a fireplace surrounded by gray glass tile. Yet the most impressive sight lay beyond the open glass wall that revealed the panoramic view of the blue backlit pool, centered between two stone walls, and the Mediterranean Sea, which stretched out as far as the eye could see.

"Amazing," Kira said. "An absolute paradise."

"I am pleased that you are pleased," Tarek replied from behind her.

Pleasure wasn't her goal, a fact she had to remember before she let the atmosphere cloud her common sense. "I'm ready to work when you are," she said as she faced him.

"Tonight we will relax and simply enjoy each other's company."

That could involve going somewhere she didn't want to go. Correction. She shouldn't go. "I slept the entire trip, Tarek. I have no problem getting started on my duties."

"We will begin first thing in the morning with a visit to the resort. In the meantime, I will show you to your room, where you can freshen up before dinner."

She saw no point in arguing with him because she couldn't deny she was starving—both for food and for his touch. She could partake in one, but not the other. Not unless she wanted to forget her reasons for being there had nothing to do with falling into bed with him again.

After Tarek started down a corridor to her right, Kira followed behind him past several rooms, all the while recalling his perfect butt, which she unfortunately couldn't see now, due to the length of his gray jacket. But she had seen that tempting bottom before in all its glory, and his well-toned legs, his ridged abdomen and his impossibly broad shoulders. She remembered in great detail clinging to those shoulders before running her palms down his back, exploring the pearls of his spine before spanning the width of his rib cage, then traveling down to the curve of his buttocks and curving her hand between his thighs…

"I hope you find it to your liking."

Kira snapped back into reality when she realized

Tarek had opened the door to a room. Stepping forward, she peered inside to find her luggage resting on a copper bench at the foot of the king-sized bed covered in a silky white spread, and another set of glass doors leading out onto a private veranda dotted with aqua chaises and white wicker tables. And yet again, another stellar view of the ocean and a private beach.

"It's definitely to my liking," she said as she stepped into the suite. "But are you sure I'm not putting you out of your room?"

Tarek moved to her side, barely two inches separating them. "My quarters are on the opposite side of the house."

Too bad—her first thought. *A good thing*—her second. At least she wouldn't have to run into him on a regular basis, should she choose that course. Right now, after catching a whiff of his heady cologne mixed with the salty scent of the sea, she would like to do more than *run* into him.

Clearing the uncomfortable hitch in her throat, she turned to him and smiled. "Is there a bathroom nearby where I can take a quick shower before dinner?"

"As you wish," he said after making a sweeping gesture toward two bifold doors.

Kira followed his lead and peeked into the spa-like bathroom, equipped with a copper-tiled shower that had enough room and spray heads to wash an army all at once. And beside that behemoth shower, a jetted soaker tub butted up against a narrow window, which provided another incredible view of water and wide-open sky. "I suppose I can make do with this."

Finally, Tarek gave her a half grin. "If it is not up to your standards, you are welcome to use my facilities. As I believe I mentioned, I have a steam shower as well as a sauna."

Getting naked anywhere near this gorgeous man would be a recipe for danger. Sensual, hot danger.

Determined to put some space between them, she moved to the white marble vanity and ran her hand over the countertop. "Actually, I was joking. It's so huge I'm afraid I might seriously get lost in here. If I don't show up in an hour, please send a search party."

"Should you go missing for any length of time, I would not want the staff to see you in a state of undress. Therefore, I would seek you out since I have already seen you naked." Before she could respond, Tarek began backing to the door. "I will inform the chef to have dinner prepared in one hour."

"All right," she said. "Where do you want me to go?"

He sent her a smoldering look that seared her from forehead to feet and all parts in between. "I fear if I answer that with complete honesty, you will not join me for our meal this evening."

She frowned. "Where exactly is the dining room?"

"You will find it beneath the stars."

With that, he exited the bath, leaving Kira alone entertaining fantasies she had no good cause to have. She immediately returned to the bedroom to unpack her suitcase and select something to wear. After her lingerie was tucked into a drawer, she stuffed the bottle of prenatal vitamins beneath it, determined not to give away her secret before she had a chance to reveal it to the master of the house. *If* she revealed it. That still remained to be seen.

She then withdrew a lightweight, sleeveless violet dress from the clothing someone had already hung in the wardrobe and selected silver bangle bracelets with matching hoop earrings from the jewelry bag in her overnight case. A fitting choice for a romantic evening. She suddenly slammed on the mental brakes following that ill-advised thought. She wasn't looking for romance. She was on a fact-finding mission involving the prospective father of her child. She didn't want moonlight and roses. She wanted to remain grounded. She didn't need to be starry-eyed. She needed to see the real Tarek Azzmar clearly.

She also had to shower quickly in order to get something in her stomach before she became queasy, just another reminder of the baby growing inside her. Hopefully she wouldn't give anything away by eating like she hadn't eaten in a month.

Kira's appetite both surprised and pleased Tarek greatly. During their dinner on the veranda, she had consumed the majority of the cheese and olive appetizers, as well as the entire Greek salad, and had left only a scarce bit of the moussaka before pushing her plate aside.

He leaned back and studied her euphoric face. "Did you save room for dessert?"

She dabbed at her mouth with the black cloth napkin and sighed. "Heavens no. If I eat anything else, I won't be able to move."

When the server brought out a tray of baklava, Tarek

waved him away. "That will be all, Alexios. Tell Leda she has done an excellent job, as usual."

When the man nodded and scurried away, Kira turned her attention to the sky. "It's such a beautiful night."

The evening had nothing on her beauty. He strayed from decorum to glimpse her breasts, which were enhanced by the low neckline of her dress. He had not remembered them being so full, but on that evening when they'd made love, he had not taken enough time to inspect them. Perhaps he would have the opportunity to remedy that. Perhaps he would be fortunate enough to use his mouth on them, the tip of his tongue to...

"My eyes are up here, Tarek."

He had been caught red-handed stealing a questionable look. "My apologies. I was simply admiring your neck. I did not notice how delicate it is until you cut your hair."

"And you are an incredibly bad liar."

Luckily she had chastised him with a smile—a cynical one. "As you have pointed out in the past, I am a man with normal desires."

"Obviously you're a breast man."

Breasts, legs, buttocks. "I admire all aspects of the female body. I consider it a work of art." And if he could capture on canvas the way she looked now—her hair ruffling in the breeze, her slender hand supporting her cheek, her mesmerizing eyes—he would be a renowned artist, not a businessman.

"Speaking of art, do you think we could visit a museum while we're here? Or maybe make a trip to see the Tombs of the Kings?"

She was a master at changing the subject. Almost as good as he. "If time allows. I have much to do to ready the resort for its grand opening before summer's end. I hope that you will assist me in the endeavor."

Her frown did not take away from her beauty. "Surely you're not all work and no play."

He would gladly carve out time to play with her. "When it involves business, I am single-minded."

She leaned back and picked up her glass. "So you hang out in this house when you're not working? Not that there would be anything wrong with hanging out here. I mean, it's a beautiful place. How long have you owned it?"

"I do not own it. I have been leasing it the past eighteen months."

"That must be costly."

"Twenty thousand euros per month."

She sputtered on the water before quickly recovering. "You might as well buy it at that cost."

"If that is what you wish, consider it done."

Now she looked perplexed. "Why would you make such a large purchase based on my opinion?"

He had actually made an offer to the owner not long ago. "I would like to believe you might return with me in the future. Solely a pleasure trip of course, with ample time to *play*."

Kira rimmed her fingertip around the edge of the glass, inadvertently causing a tightening in his groin. "You're getting ahead of yourself, aren't you? We're not certain how well we will get along in the next two weeks."

He had no doubt they would get along well, at least from a physical standpoint. "If my memory serves me correctly, we spent quite a bit of time together since our first meeting. We have engaged in several enlightening conversations."

"Yet during those times, we talked about world politics and the weather, but not once did you mention anything about your upbringing."

With good reason. "I told you I grew up in Morocco and both my parents are deceased."

"What were your parents like?"

"They were decent people." He could say that with honesty about the man who raised him, yet he had his doubts about his mother after learning of her indiscretions.

"Do you have any siblings?" she asked.

That possibility was still open to verification, and something he was not prepared to divulge. "Would you like to take a swim?"

She sighed. "Would you like for once to tell me a little bit about yourself that doesn't involve your portfolio?"

To do so could create suspicion if he made one slip of the tongue. "I would prefer to spend the rest of the evening partaking of the pool."

"I don't want to get my hair wet since I just washed it."

"Perhaps a walk on the beach?"

"In the dark?"

"The full moon will guide us."

She pushed her chair back and stood. "Definitely a walk on the beach. And while we're at it, you can tell me exactly what you're hiding."

Four

After discarding their shoes, they walked along the gray-sand shoreline side by side, without touching or speaking. Kira waited for a time for Tarek to break the silence and when he didn't, she took the initiative. "It's so peaceful here."

"Yes, it is," he replied without looking at her.

She opted to continue with lighter conversation in hopes of drawing him out. "When I was in college, we traveled to Barbados during summer break."

"We?"

He sounded oddly suspicious. "Yes. Myself and my former fiancé. His family owned a condo there. He had the entire place to himself the majority of the summer months because his parents preferred Europe."

"The man who wounded you," he said in a simple statement of fact. "He must have been wealthy."

She would provide some insight into that doomed love affair, but only a little. "Actually, he was a sultan's son from Saudi attending university in Canada. We were both in the hotel management program. Since I could speak Arabic, we made a connection, dated for a couple of years and became engaged before we broke up."

"Why did you part ways?"

She should have known he would ask and she would really rather not go into too much detail. That would completely ruin the mood. "Incompatibility."

"I thought you were a champion of honesty."

"I'm telling the truth."

"Only a partial truth. Was he unfaithful?"

She'd never found any proof of that, but there had been plenty of rumors before and after their breakup. "Look, I'd really rather not talk about it."

He paused and faced her. "I suspect he did have other women."

All the bitter memories came rushing back like the nearby waves hitting the shore. "Not that I was aware of at the time. If you must know, he found out that aside from the King of Bajul paying for my education, I had no blood ties to the royal family, so he cut me off completely. In other words, I wasn't good enough for him."

He sent her an oddly stern look. "The king financed your education?"

"Yes, out of appreciation for my parents' years of

service in the palace. He was a very generous man and like a second father to me."

When Tarek muttered something unflattering in Arabic, Kira's inquisitiveness kicked into overdrive. "Did you have some sort of falling out with King Aadil?"

"I never met the man nor did I ever attempt to meet him. However, I did not always agree with his archaic policies. I have already heard rumors regarding infidelity."

Her inherent loyalty to the Mehdis spurred her anger and she couldn't help but wonder if maybe he knew something about Adan's birth mother, Elena. Regardless, she didn't dare bring that up in case he didn't. "Talk is cheap, Tarek. Rumors are just that, rumors."

"I have often found they hold a modicum of truth, especially when repeated by many."

"Yet none of that stopped you from doing business with his sons."

"They are from a more progressive generation, and the water conservation project is a good investment."

His continuing focus on money disturbed Kira and reminded her of why they might not make a good match in the long run. As if he'd ever acted like he wanted anything more than an occasional conversation and some slap-and-tickle sessions. "I still find it a bit extreme to build a mini-palace in Bajul so you can oversee that project."

"I own houses in many places, including a villa in Barbados."

Of course he did. She saw the revelation as a means

to lighten the mood and move back into the present. "Do you visit the island often?"

"No, I do not," he said gruffly as he began to walk again. "I rarely have time for leisure."

So much for lightening the mood. She had to quicken her steps to keep up with him and with his long-legged gait, she might find herself having to sprint. "Are you angry at me because I happened to respect and like the former king, despite his faults?"

He stopped again and stared straight ahead, giving her a good glimpse of his stellar profile. "That is not my concern. I am displeased that you seem determined to dissect my past."

Her instincts had always been relatively good, leading her to believe she might be on the right track in regard to his secrets. "It's only because you seem so guarded about your life."

"As I have told you, I value my privacy. It is at times difficult to retain that privacy in light of my work."

That she could understand, but still… "All right. Keep your secrets and your privacy. It's neither here nor there whether you're open about your life, even when I just opened up about mine. Just remember, that doesn't bode well for building a true friendship."

He sent her a quick glance. "Perhaps I do not wish to be your friend."

For some reason, that stung her to the core. "Fine. We'll keep this strictly business since candor clearly isn't your strong suit."

He turned and took her by the shoulders. "If you require candor, then I will give that to you. I wish to be your lover again."

"Tarek, I—"

He pulled her closer, effectively quelling her protest. "I want to kiss you again, be inside you again, and I sense you want that as well."

Oh, how she did want that, but... "You're making this hard on me."

"You have made this *hard* on me in every sense of the word." He proved that point by moving her hand slowly, slowly down to his distended fly before sliding her palm back to his chest. "Seeing you tonight in that dress, watching you now and the way your hair ruffles in the breeze, only causes me to desire you more."

"You're trying to distract me from asking too many questions," she said, her voice sounding somewhat strained.

He brushed feathered kisses across her neck until his lips came to rest beneath her ear. "I am attempting to be candid."

"You promised you wouldn't do this." The lack of conviction in her tone, her inability to push him away, demonstrated her waning determination to resist him.

"I said I would *try* not to do this." He softly kissed her cheek. "Or this." Then he pressed his lips against hers, once, twice, before taking her mouth completely.

Kira internally debated the foolishness of giving in to him, all the while actively participating in that kiss. She readily accepted the gentle stroke of his tongue against hers, his palms roving down her back, the rush of damp heat when he pressed his erection against her pelvis. *Exactly what happened the last time*, she thought as he began to work her dress up to slide his hands inside the back of her panties. He kneaded her bottom, continued to press against her, as their kiss became deeper, more frenzied. If she didn't stop him now, they'd be making love not on marble, but on a bed of sand.

With all the strength she could muster, Kira broke the kiss and backed away, her respiration and nerves both ragged. "Tarek, we can't."

He swiped a palm over his nape. "Believe me, we could. In a matter of seconds."

"This isn't what I want." This wasn't what she had planned.

He narrowed his dark eyes and stared at her. "You are saying you do not want me?"

If she said that, she would be handing him a giant fib. "It's not about whether I want you or not. I just don't want to make a mistake I'll regret."

"Then you believe our need for each other is truly a mistake."

He had no idea how severe a mistake they'd made due to that desire. "I believe it's unwise to answer it again."

"Then I shall escort you back to your quarters," he said in a tone that revealed a hint of dejection mixed with irritation.

As they headed back to the house in silence, Kira couldn't deny her disappointment. On one hand, she did want to experience that intimacy with him again. On the other, she needed to maintain a clear head in order to establish if he was suitable to be involved in her child's future. If he would even want to step into the fatherhood role. She had no doubt that he would support their baby monetarily, but not necessarily emotionally. She refused to settle for less, even if it meant walking away from him for good.

Once they arrived at her room, Kira felt the need to say something to soothe his obviously wounded ego. "I really did enjoy our evening, Tarek, and I want you to know that any woman would be flattered to have your attention."

"But not you."

"Of course I'm flattered. I'm simply being cautious. Before I even consider being with you again, I have to be certain I'm not going to be hurt."

His features relaxed somewhat. "If you recall, we both agreed that our relationship would remain casual with no complications. What has changed?"

Everything. "I suppose I've learned I'm not the kind of woman who can engage in casual sex. I have to have more."

Now he looked concerned, as if his fight-or-flight reflex had kicked in. "How much more?"

"I need someone who appreciates me for who I am. I need to know that I'm not only a fling."

He swiped one hand over his jaw. "My lifestyle has not allowed me to consider settling into a serious re-lationship."

"Don't you want to someday have a wife and children?" She sounded almost desperate, even to her own ears.

He took both her hands into his. "I refuse to make

empty promises to you for the sake of having you in
my bed. Yet since that night, I have thought of nothing aside from you. Nevertheless, if you cannot accept
what I can offer to you at this point in time, an attentive lover who will treat you the way you deserve to
be treated, with great care, then say so now and I shall
not bother you again."

Not at all what she needed to hear. "You mean you
want sex with no strings attached."

"Life is very brief. I endeavor to make the best of
each moment. What better way to do that than to spend
those moments with a remarkable woman?"

She leaned back against the wall next to the open
door. "Are you trying to sway me to your side with
pretty words?"

"Never doubt my sincerity where you are concerned.
You are a remarkable woman. Highly intelligent and
innately sensual. Your former lover was a fool not to
recognize those attributes."

Common sense told her to let him go immediately.
The child growing in her belly said she couldn't right
now. Yet the loudest voice in her head came from her
heart. The same voice that had cautioned her during all
their lengthy conversations and heady flirtations—she
could easily fall in love with him.

She would keep that voice quieted for the time being.
"I understand what you're asking of me, and I can only
promise I'll sleep on it." If she was in fact able to sleep
at all.

He lifted her hands, turned them over and kissed

each palm before releasing her. "And that is all I ask. I will see you early in the morning."

Perhaps in the morning, she would see things more clearly.

As soon as the limo pulled into the drive leading up to the resort, the magnitude of Tarek's wealth finally hit home for Kira.

Perfection. Absolute perfection, from the white stone facade to the elaborate dual rock water features flanking the hotel's entrance. Three floors of rooms, all containing large balconies, fanned out on both sides of what appeared to be the main lobby. The manicured landscape would be described as lush and green and tropical, laid out precisely to her father's standards. Unfortunately, she couldn't express her favorable opinions to the proprietor since he'd departed for the resort long before her, according to Alexios. She couldn't help but wonder if he'd reconsidered and decided to shelve the seduction. That should give her some relief, but in reality, it gave her a sinking feeling in the pit of her stomach that had nothing to do with the pregnancy. As silly as it seemed, a part of her wanted him to persist.

After the driver stopped beneath the portico, he rounded the limo and offered his hand to help her out. Kira strolled toward the entry, expecting to be greeted by Tarek, only to see a woman emerge from the double copper doors. A classically beautiful, dark-eyed, golden-skinned woman dressed in an impeccably tailored white linen suit. Her shoulder-length raven hair had been styled in soft waves, reminiscent of a Hollywood icon from decades ago. Her makeup was equally perfect, as was her dazzling smile that almost seemed rehearsed. "Welcome, Ms. Darzin," she said as she offered a slender hand. "I am Athena Clerides, Tarek's business associate."

The goddess-like name fit her well, Kira decided, though she found it odd Tarek had failed to mention her during their many conversations. She also felt completely underdressed in her simple pink sundress and sandals. "It's a pleasure to meet you, Ms. Clerides," she replied as she shook her hand.

"Please call me Athena." Her accent hinted at her Greek roots and so did her striking features.

"As long as you call me Kira."

"Agreed. Now, if you will follow me, we will get started on your duties."

Evidently the taskmaster sent someone else to do his dirty work. "Is Tarek not here?"

Athena opened the door wide. "He is currently working on his own project. He has instructed me to have you look over the plans for the kitchen."

At least the woman didn't seem offended by the request. "I'm not certain what I have to offer you in that regard, but I'm willing to give my opinion."

"Obviously Tarek values your opinion," she said, the first touch of acrimony in her tone. "Now if you will please follow me."

Kira complied, trailing behind Athena as they walked through the high-ceiling lobby, complete with a gigantic purple Persian rug covering polished black marble floors—reminiscent of another marble floor.

She shoved the memories away and continued to survey the area. Unlike Tarek's beach rental, the décor was much more traditional, evident from the rich wood furniture and sofas covered in red, violet and gold fabrics. They continued through a lengthy corridor to the left and paused at an opening that revealed a large space, barren aside from a stainless-steel prep station centered in the middle of the room.

"This is it," Athena announced. "Or where it will be once the kitchen is complete."

"It's definitely a blank slate," Kira said. "Do you have some sort of blueprint for the layout?"

"Of course." Athena strode to the industrial island, picked up a notebook computer and held it out to Kira. "This is the current plan."

She studied the diagram before regarding Athena again. "Only one refrigerator?"

The woman looked at Kira as if she were daft. "A large refrigerator."

She studied the plan a few more moments before regarding Athena again. "Do you intend to serve wine?"

"Yes. We will be catering to travelers from around the world."

Well-heeled travelers, no doubt. "Then I suggest you add a wine refrigerator."

"I will take that into consideration, but the cupboards are scheduled to be installed this afternoon and the appliances delivered in the morning. It would cost money to make these last-minute additions."

As if the missing mogul would care. "I'm sure Tarek has a contingency in the budget to cover any added ex-

pense if the original layout needs to be reconfigured."
Kira returned to the graphic to avoid Athena's glare.
"Will the restaurant be serving only guests, or will it
be open to the public?"

"Both."

That sent the mental wheels into a spin. "Then perhaps you should add another prep area next to the dish-
washer since you have some wasted space. My mother
always said you can never have enough room for food
preparation."

Athena actually smiled. "That is a good suggestion,
though it might not be feasible to have it here for a few
more days."

Finally, they were getting somewhere. "A few more
days shouldn't matter too much."

"Tell me, was your mother a cook?"

Kira handed the notepad back to her. "A chef. She
worked for the former king of Bajul for many years.
My father tended to the palace's gardens."

Athena lifted a thin brow. "Ah. You are the daughter of domestics."

She suddenly felt like that inadequate schoolgirl
again. A commoner among royalty. Yet she would not
let Athena's snobbery shatter her confidence. "Yes, I
am, and very proud of my heritage. So much so I am
following in their footsteps."

Athena leaned a narrow hip against the metal counter. "As a cook or a groundskeeper?"

Kira felt her internal temperature begin to rise.
"Neither, actually. I'm the director of the household in
charge of all the palace staff."

The woman's smile was entirely too snide. "How nice that your parents' humble lifestyle afforded you that position."

She felt puzzled by Athena's suddenly disagreeable demeanor, yet Kira wasn't beyond matching her condescension. "A degree in hotel management afforded me that position, as well as a recommendation from the current king."

"I see. Did the current king recommend you to Tarek?"

Every word that came out of the woman's mouth sounded like an indictment. "As a matter of fact, he requested I accompany Tarek here as a temporary assistant."

Athena looked as if she'd swallowed something sour. "Since the two of you appear to be on a first-name basis, exactly how are you assisting him?"

Kira suddenly understood the reason behind Athena's attitude. Jealousy, pure and simple. "Look, Tarek and I have socialized before and have become friends. If you're suggesting more exists between us, you're wrong." Aside from a baby, a fact that would remain hidden from this woman, and the rest of the world, for the time being. "If you have a problem working with me, then I suggest you take it up with him."

Athena's features seemed to soften somewhat. "I apologize for my suspicious nature, but I have worked alongside Tarek for many years and I know him better than most. He has an affinity for attractive women such as you."

Kira wagered Athena's and Tarek's relationship went

beyond the boardroom and into the bedroom. "How long have you been with him?"

"Eight years," she said proudly. "We have traveled the globe together, and since I am a Cypriot, I encouraged him to build this resort. Because he values and trusts my judgment, he agreed the venture would be a good investment."

Clearly Ms. Clerides had quite a bit of clout, and a very close relationship with her boss. Kira found that troubling on several levels that she would take out and analyze later. "Interesting. I'm sure you'll both be very successful in this and all your future endeavors. Is there anything else you'd like to discuss?"

Athena paused as if mulling over her response. "Yes. When did you meet Tarek?"

That Kira hadn't expected. "A little over three months ago. Why?"

Athena strolled around the table, her arms folded beneath her breasts. "That does explain his recent behavior."

"I don't understand."

She paused and leveled her gaze on Kira. "I suspected he had found another woman who had captured his interest. I do believe that woman is you."

Denial seemed the best course in this case. "I'm sure you're mistaken."

"I can assure you I am not." Athena hesitated a moment, as if again carefully considering her words. "I began to notice a change in him on his return trips from Bajul over the past few months. He seemed distant and distracted, when he has always been very attentive to me."

The truth about their relationship had now been officially confirmed, as far as Kira was concerned. "Excuse my intrusiveness, but I assume you and Tarek are lovers."

Athena appeared somewhat chagrined. "We *were* lovers until three months ago. He told me that our relationship had run its course and he was freeing me to pursue other options."

Unmistakable hurt filtered out in Athena's tone, leaving Kira in a quandary over what to say next. "I'm sorry it didn't work out since you obviously care about him."

Athena lifted her shoulders in a shrug. "Tarek is not the type of man who embraces a serious relationship. However, he is magnetic and very seductive, which affords him the ability to make a woman discard her convictions, along with her clothes. I caution you to keep that in mind."

Too late for that. "As I've said, Tarek and I are only friends."

"The heightened color on your face says otherwise."

Kira hated that her annoying blush gave away her feelings like a digital billboard. "Necessary or not, I will certainly take your caution to heart."

"And that will better enable you to protect your heart." She hesitated before adding, "Have you asked him about the phone calls?"

"Phone calls?"

"The one he makes every afternoon at the same time."

She hadn't been around him long enough to notice. "No, I haven't."

"Then pay attention and you will soon see it is part of his routine, and a mystery."

"Are you inferring he's speaking with a woman?"

"I suspected he is, but he has never been forthcoming. In all the years I've been with him, the identity of the party on the other end of the line remains a mystery. Perhaps you will be the one to solve it."

She had a few qualms about that. Tarek Azzmar might forever be an enigma. And if only she'd received Athena's counsel before that night six weeks ago. If Tarek rejected their baby, she would be heartbroken. "I suppose you should point me in the direction of Tarek now."

"You will most likely find him in the courtyard."

"That was certainly awkward, Tarek." And so was seeing him dressed in white painter's pants, sans shirt, displaying smooth warm skin on his remarkably strong back. He continued to carefully lay gray stone into the beginnings of a feature wall near the unfilled swimming pool, apparently too engrossed to respond to her comment.

Please don't turn around, she thought as he continued to go about his task, while she continued to shamelessly study his amazing physique. Much to her dismay, he failed to heed her silent request and faced her, showing to full advantage his ruffled hair, unshaven jaw, the slight shading on his newsworthy chest, the flat plane of his abdomen. Her gaze immediately came to rest on his navel, which was exposed by the low-slung waistband on the pants, before returning to his face. Of course, she immediately focused on his mouth.

After grabbing a rag from the nearby work table, he wiped his hands, then whipped out a scowl. "What is this awkwardness you speak of?"

For a moment, Kira couldn't remember what she had said when she'd come upon him looking like one hundred percent prime male. Fortunately, she recovered quickly when she recalled her tense conversation with his ex-girlfriend. "I don't appreciate you sending me into the lion's den with the lioness."

"Please explain."

Oh, she would. Gladly. "You should have informed me that you and Athena were lovers."

He tossed the rag aside and put on a somber expression. "She informed you of this?"

"Yes, because she assumes I'm her replacement."

He went back to cutting another stone. "And you said?"

"She was mistaken. She also warned me that you are the consummate heartbreaker."

That earned her another frown. "I prefer not to discuss this here."

Maybe not here. Maybe not now. But they would discuss it tonight.

Kira brought her attention to the intricacy of the wall and realized Tarek had talents she hadn't known about until then. In reality, she still knew very little about him from a personal standpoint, even if she did know what he looked like naked.

"Where did you learn to do this?"

He placed another tile—this one rust-colored—into the pattern. "I was schooled by the man who raised me."

"You mean your father?"

"Yes."

"Then why didn't you say that?"

He glanced at her over one shoulder. "He is the man who raised me, is he not?"

"Yes, but…" No need to argue a point she wouldn't win. "Was this a hobby, or did he make a living as a stone mason?"

"A meager living," he said as he faced her again. "His craft sent him to an early grave."

She could imagine the poor man being trapped under a stone wall. "Did he suffer a work-related injury?"

"He suffered from a weak heart that claimed him before his fiftieth birthday, as it was with his own father."

Kira's palm automatically went to her belly, an unexpected maternal gesture. "That probably causes you quite a bit of concern in regard to your own health."

"It does not."

In her opinion, he should be worried, yet Tarek would forever be a tough guy in her eyes. When it came to their child, she couldn't help but be troubled by genetic predisposition to disease. "What happened to your mother?"

His expression turned somber, as if he had been plagued by sudden and unwelcome memories. "She contracted pneumonia the year I turned ten and never recovered. She suffered from a weak will."

Kira swallowed around her shock. "That's a crass thing to say about the woman who gave birth to you."

"It is the truth, according to her husband. I barely remember her beyond a few select memories."

Odd that he couldn't seem to say "father." A very telling omission, and perhaps the reason behind his inability to commit. Maybe his father cheated on his mother. Maybe the man had been cold and distant. She could only hope that someday she would find out.

"I'm sure it's difficult to get past the grief over losing both parents so soon in life. I don't know what I would do without mine."

Tarek swept the back of one arm over his forehead now beaded with perspiration. "I am glad you enjoyed a stable childhood. Now if you will excuse me, I will finish here and see you at the villa later."

Talk about being dismissed in short order. She refused to let him get away with it the next time they conversed. "Fine. Hopefully you'll be back by lunchtime."

Five

The sun had long since set before Tarek returned home. The troubling conversation with Kira had prompted him to remain longer in an effort to discard the bitter memories. In an effort to avoid her questions.

He had loved his mother greatly and had mourned her loss as any other devoted son would. He had respected her without fail...until he had learned of her deception and indiscretions. Since gaining that knowledge, he had concentrated on rising above his upbringing, and avoiding interpersonal relationships. He had built a financial empire that rivaled most. He had achieved this virtually alone.

Tonight, he would push those recollections away and concentrate on the one woman who could help him forget, if she would be willing to do that. To attain his goal, he would endeavor to answer her questions, at least those that he could answer. And perhaps he would ask a few questions of her.

After he entered the foyer, a person walking toward the end of the pool, cast in blue shadows, caught his attention. The curve of her hips and the grace of her movements left no question as to her gender. He had explored those curves before, and he wished to do so again. First, he must find out if she was still speaking to him.

After she executed a perfect dive and began to swim the length of the pool, Tarek strode through the open glass doors, claimed a nearby chair and waited for her to take notice of his appearance. He continued to wait an interminable amount of time until his patience began to wane. Before he could call Kira's name, she finally paused, climbed up the steps on the opposite end of the pool, grabbed a towel from a table and began drying off…slowly.

The swimsuit she wore barely covered her breasts and bottom, revealing a body designed to drive a man to the brink of insanity. He could not determine if she had yet to detect his presence, or if she was simply ignoring him. Regardless, he continued to watch her slide the towel down her thighs, well aware of what his perusal was doing to his libido. The pressure began to build until a painful erection strained behind his fly.

"I see you finally decided to come home."

Her comment thrust him out of his sexual trance, yet did nothing to remedy his current predicament. "My apologies for my tardiness. The time got away from me and then I had to shower and change before returning." He could use another shower now, if only to quell his lust.

After securing the towel low on her hips, Kira joined him and took the chair next to his. "Did you have dinner?"

"I did."

"With Athena?"

And so began the interrogation. "No. I dined alone at a small bistro near the resort. I assume you have eaten."

She rested against the back of the chair, revealing a clear view of her bare flesh, from her breasts to where the towel split at her thighs, adding fuel to the fire burning in his groin. "Yes, I did. A nice seafood salad, which I ate alone, too."

Touché. "Again, I apologize for not being here to share the meal with you."

"I'll accept your apology only if you're willing to explain a few things to me."

"I will try." That explanation could require several half-truths.

"What exactly is your relationship with Athena?"

"We have a business relationship. That is all."

"But it hasn't always been that way, Tarek. How serious were you?"

"Our liaison was solely for convenience. We spent quite a bit of time together and made the most of our proximity. Aside from that, there was no talk of permanency."

She swept a hand through her hair. "You might want to inform her of that."

"Athena has always known my expectations."

"Maybe, but did you know she's in love with you?"

He had suspected as much, though she had never said. "Athena loves the challenge and the chase. If I have wounded her, it would be limited to her pride."

She released a cynical laugh. "For such a smart man, you know very little about women."

"I admit women are enigmas, yet I do know Athena well."

"Apparently not if you haven't noticed all the signs leading to the aforementioned love aspect."

He was growing increasingly uncomfortable over the course of the conversation. "If you are referring to emotional entanglement, we agreed that would not be included when we became intimate."

"Tarek, most women are not wired like men. At times we're slaves to our emotions. That can lead to that most dreaded emotion, love."

"Love defies logic."

She sighed. "Love isn't supposed to be logical. It's about caring so much for someone you can't envision your life without them. Of course, a logical man like yourself probably has no clue what I'm talking about."

If she only knew the effort it required to reject those emotions, and how long it had taken to banish them from his life. "I am not without compassion, Kira, yet I am determined to keep grounded in order to succeed in life."

She appeared to be growing impatient with him. "You mean succeed at business, don't you, Tarek? Here's a headline. Life isn't only about building fabulous resorts, one larger than the other, to pay homage to the money gods. If you can't enjoy the fruits of your labor with someone you care about, what good is all the money in the world?"

"It is not only about the monetary gains. It involves the challenge of achieving a goal."

She came to her feet and released the towel again. "Speaking of challenges, I have a few more laps to swim."

"I will join you," he said as he stood.

"Knock yourself out, although I might be finished with my swim by the time you change." With that, she strode to the end of the pool and dove in.

He saw a way to remedy the lack of time, though it could cost him if Kira did not approve. He believed it to be worth the risk, and possibly rewarding.

After he toed out of his shoes and removed his socks, he quickly took off his shirt, slacks and boxer briefs. Kira continued to swim laps, presumably unaware he was completely nude when he dove into the pool. He swam to the shallow end near the steps to wait for her to reach him. Once she did, he clasped her wrist and brought her into his arms.

"What are you doing?" she asked as she pushed her hair away from her face.

"I am concerned you are exerting yourself too much."

"I'll be the judge of that, and how did you change so fast? Were you wearing your trunks under your pants?"

"I preferred not to waste time changing."

Awareness dawned in her expression. "You're naked."

He could not contain a smile. "Perhaps."

She reached around him and ran her palm over his bare buttock. "You really enjoy being the bad boy, don't you?"

"Perhaps," he repeated. "I am good at it."

She rolled her eyes. "Yes, you are. Do you mind if I get back to swimming now?"

He brushed a kiss across her cheek. "I can think of a more enjoyable way to exert ourselves."

When he kissed her neck, she murmured, "This isn't fair."

He suspected she would bring out the friendship-only argument. "It is fair because this is what we both want. I can tell by the way you are trembling."

"It's not fair because you're seducing a hormone-ridden woman."

Far be it for him to question that. He was simply thankful his theory had been wrong, encouraging him to proceed. He rimmed his tongue around the shell of her ear and whispered, "And I am a hormone-ridden man." He then took a major chance, took her hand and pressed her palm against his erection. "I want you desperately."

"I see your point," she said in a breathy tone. "Or maybe I should say I feel your point."

When Kira began to stroke him, Tarek realized he could not retain control if he did not stop her. He mustered all his strength, swept her into his arms and set her on the pool's edge. He kissed her then, slowly yet insistently, as he untied the string around her neck and unclasped the strap at her back. He waited for her protest and when she did not, he tossed the bikini top behind him and moved his mouth to her breast. As he circled his tongue around her nipple, she clasped his head and released a soft moan. As he moved his attention to her other breasts, she uttered, "I'm going to hate myself for this in the morning."

The comment proved as effective as frigid water on Tarek's libido. He refused to continue foreplay with an unwilling woman.

On that thought, he stood and ascended the steps, leaving her sitting there, her mouth agape. "What are you doing?"

He grabbed the towel and tossed it to her, then began gathering his clothes. "I am retiring to bed."

After covering herself in cloth, she climbed out of the pool and approached him. "Quite frankly, I don't appreciate you working me into a sexual frenzy, then stopping without any explanation."

After setting his clothing aside on the table, he pulled on his underwear to cover the fact he was not quite recovered. "As much as I would like to make love to you again, I cannot in good conscience continue and, in turn, be the reason for your regrets in the morning."

She sighed. "It's very difficult for me to fight this, but I don't want to complicate our situation more by making a wrong decision."

"Our situation does not have to be complicated. We are two vital people who enjoy intimacy."

She sent him a frustrated look. "But what happens

after we return to Bajul? Do we pretend our first night together and this trip didn't exist?"

Truth be known, he could not tolerate the thought of not seeing her again. He found her intriguing, fascinating, and since their meeting, she had never been a thought away in his mind. Yet he feared he could never measure up to her ideal of what a man should be.

"I would be remiss if I made promises to you that I cannot keep at this point in my life. Knowing that, should you decide you would like to explore further intimacy, I would welcome that decision. Consequently, you may rest assured I will not pursue you again."

"All right," she said as she started away then paused to face him again. "If you're okay with forgetting what transpired between us, so be it. But I, on the other hand, will carry the reminders with me for years."

After Kira disappeared into the house, Tarek dropped down on a chaise to ponder the puzzling comment. He despised the thought that he had wounded her so deeply that she would forever have his careless disregard imprinted on her soul. He hated that he had not seen through her guise about accepting a casual relationship. She still retained a certain amount of innocence, whereas he had become jaded when matters of the heart were involved.

He needed to stay away from her, yet never touching her again seemed unthinkable. More important, she had begun to stir emotions he wanted to ignore. Perhaps he could not love her for the long term, but he could find some way to prove that he was not the ogre she believed him to be. That he did value her. He would have to achieve that objective without a hint of seduction, and that mission would prove to be quite the challenge.

"He wants me to do what?"

Athena walked into the private elevator leading to the third floor and waited for Kira to enter and the doors to close before responding. "Tarek has asked that you select the finishes for the owner's suite."

Of all the strange requests. "Shouldn't he be doing that? Better still, shouldn't you? After all, you know him better than I do."

"One would think," Athena said. "But he insists you should take charge of this."

From Athena's slightly acid tone, Kira could tell the woman wasn't the least bit happy. "Fine, but I would really appreciate your input as well."

"My pleasure," she said as she threw open the wooden double doors with dramatic flair. "Here we are."

Kira stepped inside the massive suite, which was well lit due to the bank of glass doors, much like those back at the villa. The view of the surf hitting the private beach below was no less impressive. Aside from a huge king-sized bed with a bare mattress and a black bureau on one wall, the room was as empty as the kitchen. At least the walls had been painted white.

Athena crossed the room and gestured Kira to the double dresser. "These are a few samples the designer left for you to review."

Kira leaned over and studied the samples, then pointed at one opaque tile. "This is out because Tarek doesn't like green."

"Perhaps you know him better than you assume."

She sent Athena a weak smile over one shoulder. "Not really. I just remember him mentioning it in passing during one of our conversations."

"I am surprised since green is often associated with money."

Kira ignored Athena's cynical tone and turned back to the samples. "I believe the gray glass tile works well for the shower, white porcelain tile for the floor and Carrara marble for the bathroom vanity. The darker bamboo for the bedroom flooring would be a nice contrast."

"I agree," Athena said, actually sounding as if she did. "What would you suggest for the color palette in the bedroom?"

When Kira straightened, her head began to spin. "I think…I need to sit down."

Looking concerned, Athena surprisingly took her by the shoulders and sat her down on the bed. "May I get you something?"

"Some water," Kira croaked as she waited for the dizziness to subside.

"Did you have breakfast?" Athena asked.

She shook her head. "I had some pineapple juice."

"Then I will return with some proper food immediately. In the meantime, feel free to lie down."

After Athena left, Kira kicked off her sandals and stretched out on the plush mattress, one arm draped over her eyes. The lack of sleep certainly hadn't helped her predicament, nor had her and Tarek's interlude last night. She'd come so close to telling him about the baby, yet she'd lost her courage at the last minute. Maybe the time had come to let him in on the secret. Or not. She needed more time, a better opportunity. A more private place where they would be guaranteed privacy. She couldn't imagine anything worse than to have someone walk in on them when she was saying, "Oh by the way, Tarek, I'm going to have a baby...."

"Are you not well, Kira?"

Speaking of the prospective daddy. She uncovered her eyes to see Tarek standing at the footboard, holding a glass of water. "I'm fine. I didn't sleep well last night."

He rounded the bed, perched on the edge of the mattress and offered her the glass. "Perhaps you should return to the villa to rest."

Kira scooted up against the headboard and took a sip of water. "I've barely done anything today aside from picking out a few tiles, which leads me to a question. Why do you want me to decorate your suite?"

"I value your judgment."

"I still believe you should provide your input, in case I'm off base."

"As long as it is not green, I will be satisfied with your choices."

"You spoke to Athena."

He cracked a half smile. "How else would I have learned of your illness?"

"I'm not ill, Tarek. I'm...." She couldn't tell him here, or now for that matter. She needed more time to prepare. More time to know if telling him would be the right move to make. "I'm just a little fatigued."

Fortunately, he didn't look skeptical, but he did look

concerned. "Then you should definitely return to the house to rest. However, I do have a task for you this evening if you are feeling up to it. One I believe you will enjoy."

Task could cover a whole spectrum of possibilities.

"I'm positive I'll be fine by then. I do have a question, though. Does this task require wearing all our clothes?"

He hesitated, leading Kira to believe he was warring with himself over a proper response. "Yes, it does. Dress in formal attire and meet me at the entry no later than nine p.m."

Kira experienced a nip of panic over eating that late, and not having a thing to wear. "I brought only a few casual outfits and business suits."

He came to his feet and held out his hand. "Then I shall have something appropriate sent to the villa. Do you have a color preference?"

She allowed him to help her up, but continued to grip the water glass with both hands to quell the urge to touch him. "I'm sure I'll be happy with what you pick, and I'm almost certain it won't be green."

His smile arrived full-throttle, bright as the sun and sensual to a fault. "I will have Athena choose the dress."

Lovely. That meant she could be wearing metallic rags. "All right. Can you give me a hint as to what we'll be doing this evening?"

"I will say only that you will have a memorable experience."

Knowing him, and herself in his presence, she had no doubt about that.

* * *

"Exactly how well do you know Kira Darzin?"

Seated in his private office at the resort, Tarek continued to scan the expense report, intent on ignoring Athena's inquisition. "I see we've gone over budget on the kitchen redesign."

"Your newest protégée is to blame for that. I ask again, how well do you know her?"

He set the binder aside on the desk and leaned back in his chair. "She is not my protégée. She is serving as my advisor."

Athena began to pace the room like a captive animal. "I have known you to be a lot of things when it comes to women, but never naïve."

"What is your point, Athena?"

She paused to face him, her hands tightly balled at her sides. "I believe she is bent on sabotaging you by insisting on unnecessary changes to the resort's plans. Everything she has suggested will cost you more money."

Athena was more ruthless than he when it came to expenditures, even though it did not affect her bank account. "Why do you believe she would do this?"

She began pacing again. "Revenge, perhaps. I suspect you have angered her and she is attempting to punish you by targeting what you cherish the most. Your fortune."

He kept a choke hold on his anger. "These accusations you are making are absurd, Athena. The price of the alterations to the original kitchen configuration is minimal in light of the overall cost to build this resort. Your allegations stem from a personal vendetta."

She appeared shocked by his assessment. "I have no idea why you would believe that."

"Kira mentioned that you confirmed we were lovers. Perhaps this attack on her motivation is your retribution for the wrongs you believe I have committed against you."

"And your indictment tells me that this woman matters more to you than you care to admit. And since you have such faith in Ms. Darzin's abilities, perhaps it would be best if I resign my position, effective immediately."

Tarek shoved his chair back and stood. "You would leave in the middle of a project you encouraged me to begin?"

"Actually, yes. I'm certain you and your new charge will work very well together, until you tire of her as you tired of me."

He refused to wage a war of words with her. "I will see to it you receive suitable severance for your efforts."

Athena's smile was laced with sarcasm. "How generous of you. And as soon as you take off your blinders, you might want to pay more attention to your new lover's behavior. She could very well be harboring a secret that would not please you."

Before Tarek could offer a rejoinder, Athena rushed out of the room like a tempest and slammed the door behind her. He knew how Athena operated when she did not have her way. She would attempt to come back, apologize and return to business as usual. This time, he would not take her back, nor would he give any credence to her suspicions. He would sense if Kira was hiding something important from her. Unlike Athena, she did not have a deceptive cell in her being. She had demonstrated that to him through her insistence he be completely honest with her, and he had yet to answer that request.

No matter. He was more than ready to sever all ties with Athena, despite the hardship it would create on their deadline. This turn of events would change all aspects of his current project, yet he felt optimistic he had the answer to the dilemma—as long as he could demonstrate to Kira how much he needed her.

She needed to finish putting on her makeup, but first she needed to answer the summons.

As she tightened her white terry bathrobe, Kira crossed the room and opened the door to Alexios, who was clutching a vinyl garment bag. "Your attire for the evening, madam," he said.

She couldn't wait to see what Athena had picked out and, in some ways, dreaded it. "Thank you, Alexios. And tell Ms. Clerides I appreciate her assistance in choosing the dress."

He sent her a puzzled look. "Mr. Azzmar selected the attire, not Miss Clerides."

Even more intriguing. Apparently the rebuffed ex-lover had intentionally declined making the purchase. "I see. I'll thank him later. Is he here now?"

"He is currently placing his routine call to Morocco. He told me to inform you he will be awaiting your arrival at the entry."

"Thank you, Alexios. Tell him I shouldn't be too long."

"As you wish, Madam," he said before heading away.

Kira closed the door and pondered what the servant had said. Could that call be the one Athena had mentioned? Of course, logic said Tarek was speaking with the staff at the Moroccan mansion. Or that he had a silent business partner. Or another woman waiting in the wings.

She had no cause to be suspicious and hated that Athena had put those thoughts in her head, probably intentionally so.

Discarding her concerns for the time being, Kira laid the bag on the bed, unzipped it and removed one of the most beautiful full-length gowns she had ever seen. A shimmering fitted silver gown with a plunging halter neckline and an equally low back, along with a box containing matching high-heeled silver sandals.

She was admittedly floored by Tarek's choice and extremely surprised to find he'd chosen her correct size with both the dress and shoes. Maybe a lucky guess, but she predicted he'd had one of the staff check out her closet for reference.

After laying the gown across the bed, she returned to the bathroom to finish fixing her face, then pulled her hair back from her forehead and secured it with pins. Now for the finishing touch—putting on the one-carat diamond studs, the only souvenir from her previous relationship since she'd tossed the engagement ring at him during their breakup. Was that appropriate, wearing earrings another man had given her? Possibly not, but what Tarek didn't know wouldn't hurt him. Except for the whole baby issue.

She could spring the news on him tonight. Or not. She still needed to learn more about him, ask a few leading questions in light of what she'd recently learned, and then decide if he deserved to be a daddy. Wanted to be a daddy. The answer to both could be a resounding no.

Recognizing time was slipping away, Kira shrugged out of the robe and stepped into the dress. She then walked to the floor-length mirror hanging on the back of the door to do a closer inspection. No panty lines since she'd opted to go without them. No angle that made her butt look too big. No unsightly belly bulge. A perfect fit. A few weeks from now, she wouldn't be able to say that. A few weeks from now, her child's future would be resolved. She hoped.

She perched on the edge of the bed, slid her feet into the heels and grabbed the small black clutch. Now that she was appropriately dressed, Kira set out to find her billionaire prince and prepared to be wined and dined, minus the wine. Tonight she would pretend this fantasy date was the real deal. Tomorrow she would return to reality.

Six

"Madam, your chariot has arrived."

After Alexios moved aside, Kira stepped out the door and confronted one more pleasant surprise. Not a chariot per se, but close enough. A white carriage, attached to a matched pair of gray and white dappled horses wearing purple feather plumes and piloted by a dignified driver, sat beneath the portico. Standing beside that fancy form of transportation was a gorgeous man wearing a black tuxedo and an overtly sensual smile surrounded by a slight shading of whiskers.

Once she had the presence of mind to move, she felt as if she floated toward Tarek, caught up in some surreal, romantic fantasy. She almost asked him to pinch her when he took her hand and helped her into the carriage. She almost pinched herself to make certain she wasn't dreaming this whole unexpected scenario.

Instead, when Tarek slid into the seat next to her, Kira kissed his cheek to show her gratitude. "This is absolutely wonderful. The dress, the transportation, everything. You're definitely off to a good start, but what's next on the agenda? Perhaps a moonlit cruise on the Mediterranean?"

He slid his arm through hers, as if they were on a real date, and grinned. "You will see soon enough."

Could the man be any more cryptic? "You could at least give me a hint as to where we're going."

"The resort."

She couldn't quell the disappointment over Tarek's type-A personality. "You apparently can't begin playtime before you do a little work first."

"In a manner of speaking, we both have work to do."

Wonderful. "If that's the case, our attire is probably overkill."

"Not necessarily. You will simply have to trust me."

Oh, that she could. When she'd initially met him, she'd sensed he was a womanizer but aside from that, believed he was trustworthy, at least on a business level. Now she wasn't at all certain due to his refusal to discuss any significant details about his past, but she'd give him the benefit of the doubt until proven wrong.

Kira opted to forget her cares and take pleasure in the ride. As they made their way down the winding road leading to the resort, she relished the feel of the warm breeze blowing across her face and studied the darkening sky. She thoroughly enjoyed the scent of

Tarek's exotic cologne, which reminded her of sandalwood incense. She truly liked the fact they were so cozy in this Cinderella coach, and was concerned that she could get carried away when Tarek began stroking her bare arm.

She imagined a few other strokes in less-than-obvious places. She fantasized about throwing caution to the wind just to experience his mastery one more time. She began to wonder if she'd entirely lost her marbles, as her mother used to say.

Before she had time to ponder her sanity any further, the driver pulled up to the resort and brought the carriage to an abrupt stop by the front doors. Tarek climbed out first, took her by the waist, lifted her out and set her on her feet. Yes, she had definitely stepped into a fairy tale.

Kira waited while Tarek handed their escort a roll of bills before they headed toward the entry, his palm resting lightly on her exposed back. Even that innocent gesture had her ready and willing to climb all over him like a sheet of human shrink wrap. Boy, was she in big trouble, and the night had barely begun.

"Where to now?" she asked as they walked into the lobby.

"The ballroom."

No surprise there. "I hope you're not suggesting we have a repeat of our first night together." Actually, she hoped he was.

He sent her a half smile. "The thought had crossed my mind, but we will not be alone tonight."

Evidently he'd arranged some social soiree without her knowledge or assistance. "Who's on the guest list?"

"You will soon see."

She actually saw nothing but a table for two near the far wall of the massive room covered in—of course— a white marble floor. Her heels sounded like tap shoes as they crossed to the table, where Tarek pulled out her chair. As soon as she was seated, a somewhat rotund man dressed in a white suit and black tie strode into the room. "Madam, Monsieur, I am François and I will be serving you tonight."

Tarek claimed the chair across from Kira's and tented his hands together on the table. "Has John Paul found the kitchen satisfactory?"

François let go a boisterous laugh as he unfolded one white cloth napkin and laid it in Kira's lap. "He is very honored to be the first to use it." After he unfolded Tarek's napkin and offered it to him, he added, "I will return briefly with the opening course."

"The kitchen was completed?" Kira asked, dumb-founded, after François left.

"Not completely," Tarek said. "The preparation table you requested will not arrive until tomorrow and there are still a few finishing touches that need to be made. Otherwise, it is quite adequate for meal preparation at this time."

She bent one elbow on the table's edge and supported her cheek with her palm. "It sounds as if you've already hired your head chef."

Tarek took a drink of water from a crystal goblet then set it aside. "He is actually auditioning tonight, and so is François. They are both employed at a five-star hotel in Paris that is owned by one of my competitors. If you find the meal and service satisfactory, I will entice them both away."

Kira leaned back in the chair and sighed. "You are clearly the greatest competitor of all if you're stealing employees."

"There is no true theft involved. If the price is right, most anyone can be bought."

That didn't hold true for her. "If you say so."

François interrupted the discourse by delivering two trays brimming with appetizers that included steamed mussels and cold-boiled shrimp, along with a variety of cheeses and fruit. Kira's tummy began to rumble despite the fact she'd had two snacks since lunch. At this rate, she would require maternity clothes, or tents, by her second trimester.

Regardless, she ate with abandon the luscious fresh salad, the array of fresh vegetables and the petite filet mignon accompanied by a lobster tail. She did skip the wine, but not the sorbet designed to cleanse the palate between courses. In fact, she'd barely drawn a breath before the *pêche Melba* arrived for dessert. Spun sugar and ice cream probably wouldn't help her expanding waistline, but at least the peaches were healthy. Sort of.

When she noticed Tarek staring at her as he had the last time she'd gorged herself, her face began to flame. "I'm sorry. I'm not accustomed to eating this late, so needless to say, I was starving."

"No apology necessary," he said. "I appreciate a

woman with a healthy appetite, though I am surprised you are still quite thin."

Just wait a few weeks, she started to say but thought better of it. "Honestly, I don't normally eat so much. Something about this island atmosphere makes me very hungry."

"It fuels my appetites as well."

His usage of the plural form of "appetite," led Kira to believe he wasn't only referring to food. "Well, that definitely quenched one of mine."

He sent her a knowing and somewhat smoldering look. "Then I suppose I do not need to ask if you enjoyed the fare."

"I would think that's obvious."

They shared in a laugh, the first one she'd heard escape from Tarek's mouth since they'd been there. If he knew the reason behind her ravenous behavior, he wouldn't be laughing.

François suddenly reappeared and gathered the empty dessert cups. "John Paul has asked if you found the meal satisfactory."

"You could say that," Kira muttered. "Let him know that as the daughter of a chef, I know excellent culinary skill, and he earns high marks on all counts."

The waiter executed a slight bow and regarded Tarek. "I shall let him know. Will there be anything else, Monsieur Azzmar? Perhaps the lady would like to sample a delicate chocolate liqueur?"

"No, thank you," Kira said, perhaps a bit too abruptly.

Tarek reached into his inside pocket, withdrew two

envelopes and handed them to Francois. "Tell John Paul I will be in touch soon with my offer for both of you. I am certain he will find it more than generous. In the meantime, enjoy the rest of your stay in Cyprus."

The man practically beamed. "I assure you he will be pleased to know that, as am I. Shall I send the others in now?"

"Please do."

She hoped "others" didn't involve more food. "You don't have more chefs to audition, do you?"

"Musicians."

As soon as he said it, a group of men arrived, carrying various instruments they began to set up on a slightly elevated stage at the front of the expansive ballroom. After they took their positions, they began to play a very familiar Billie Holiday tune.

She regarded Tarek with awe. "That happens to be my grandmother's favorite song."

He favored her with a soft smile. "Then it must be kismet they chose it. Would you like to dance?"

He apparently didn't value his toes. "It's been ages since I've done that, and I'm not very good."

"I am," he proclaimed as he stood, rounded the table and pulled out her chair. "A skill I had to hone due to the many social events I have attended during the course of my career."

At least he'd qualified his sudden burst of ego. "Then I suppose I'll have to rely on you to guide me."

"That would be my pleasure."

After she took his offered hand, he led her to the dance floor and pulled her gently into his arms. Although her heels gave her an extra three inches of height, making him only five inches taller than she was, she still felt petite and protected in his embrace.

She soon realized he'd been truthful when he led her through the steps with amazing expertise. She stumbled twice and muttered, "Sorry," each time. He responded with reassuring words. Before long, they seemed as if they had danced together forever.

As the music continued, they held each other closer, and closer still when the band played a sultry jazz number that reminded Kira of hot summer nights. "Hot" was the operative word when Tarek began rubbing her back, then pressed his lips against her forehead. She felt as if she might actually go up in flames when he moved to her mouth and kissed her in earnest without regard for their audience. Frankly she didn't care, either. She only cared about the soft glide of his tongue against hers and how much she had needed this. How much she needed more. But at what cost?

When Tarek ended the kiss, she practically groaned in protest. "We should leave now."

She didn't want the night to end and knew it wouldn't if she gave him the lovemaking go-ahead when they got home. "It's still fairly early."

"Yes, and our journey is not over yet."

"Are we going to watch the staff clean up now?"

He released a low laugh. "No. We have somewhere else to go."

"Where?"

He brushed another quick kiss across her lips. "That is a surprise."

"You're certainly full of those tonight."

"This surprise happens to be the best one of all."

A yacht. A white four-level yacht moored at the exclusive marina's dock, the likes of which Kira had never seen up close and personal.

She glanced to her left to discover Tarek looked very proud of the monstrous boat. "Is this yours?"

"It is," he said as he clasped her hand to guide her up the gangplank. "And as you mentioned earlier, we will be enjoying a moonlit cruise."

Clearly she'd become clairvoyant. "That sounds like a marvelous idea." And a chance to make a few more memorable moments before she lowered the baby boom.

When they reached the entry and Tarek opened the door, a gray-haired man dressed in navy-blue military-like garb greeted them with a smile. "Good evening, Mr. Azzmar," he said, his voice hinting at an Australian accent. "You've picked a beaut of a night for a ride. Hope you brought your bathers."

"We will not be swimming tonight, Max. We will enjoy the sea from the deck."

"That you will." He aimed his grin at Kira. "Who might this lovely lady be?"

She offered her hand to the presumed captain. "I'm Kira, Mr. Azzmar's personal assistant."

Max looked her up and down. "I'd be looking for another job if my boss made me dress that way for work. Not that I'm personally complaining."

"I believe it is time to set out," Tarek said. "Otherwise we will be taking a daylight cruise."

The man's pleasant expression indicated he wasn't at all concerned with Tarek's somewhat irritable tone. "Yes, sir. We'll be off right away."

After Max ascended a staircase across the way, Kira surveyed her surroundings. To her right, a series of white leather built-in sofas butted up to a bank of windows, accompanied by black tables and nautical-themed accessories. To her left, another staircase led upstairs and one led to a lower floor, both backlit in blue with glass guardrails. Beyond that, she spied what appeared to be another living area with black high-end furniture set out on the sleek white porcelain floor. She'd learned one important fact about Tarek. He liked black and white—and that seemed to suit his personality.

"How many bedrooms and baths does this house-sized boat have?" she asked.

"Three bedrooms on the lower deck," he replied. "Six baths. One on the swim deck, one on the bridge deck, one here on the main deck, and three attached to the bedrooms."

Kira couldn't imagine having to clean six bathrooms. She couldn't imagine how much the yacht cost, either, though she suspected probably in the millions. "I haven't seen a maid yet."

"I have a staff of stewards, but they have been dismissed for the night."

"Then it's just us and Max?"

"Correct."

Essentially they were completely alone except for the captain. No one to disturb them. That both excited and worried her. The way she'd felt in his arms on the dance floor hadn't dissipated in the least. "So what now?"

"I will pour us each a glass of champagne and we will enjoy it on the aft deck."

"No champagne," she said a little more forceful than necessary.

He gave her a quizzical look. "As I recall, we shared several glasses of wine in the past."

She searched her brain for a logical excuse. "True, but I'm opting for a healthier lifestyle. Also, I put on a few pounds lately so I've decided to lay off the alcohol." Of course, the way she'd eaten in his presence would most likely lead to the conclusion she needed to lay off food in general.

"I would not have guessed you had put on any weight," he said. "But far be it for me to involve myself in a woman's decisions when it comes to personal choices."

Whew. She'd definitely dodged a bullet for now. "I would love a glass of sparkling water if you have some available."

"I do. Follow me."

As Tarek walked into the second living area, Kira trailed behind him until he paused and rounded an elaborate built-in bar with silver quartz countertops and shelves full of premier liquors. She waited nearby while he opened the stainless-steel refrigerator to retrieve a bottle of the finest champagne a large sum of money could buy. After he filled a flute with the wine, he reached beneath the bar and withdrew a green bottle of sparkling water, poured some in a high-ball glass and topped it off with two ice cubes.

He handed her the glass, along with a small napkin embossed with his initials. "I have two more bottles, should you require more."

She sipped the water, then smiled. "Usually one is my limit, but I'm feeling somewhat daring tonight, so I might have two."

He rubbed his chin and returned her smile. "Living life on the edge is my specialty."

That attitude could affect their future as parents.

"Shall we go bask in the moonlight now?"

He rounded the bar, grabbed his drink and took her hand. "Yes, and perhaps be a bit daring."

Kira wasn't certain what he meant by that, yet she sincerely wanted to find out. Clearly her hormones had commandeered her common sense. But with the feel of his slightly callused palm in hers as he showed her to the veranda, the scent of his heady cologne, that gorgeous mouth framed by a slight blanket of whiskers, taking a sensual journey with him again wouldn't be a bad thing. Or would it?

She could throw caution to the trade winds, or come back to the land of realism. He had no idea she was pregnant. And she still had no idea how to tell him. Yet when he guided her to the deck, stood behind her and wrapped one arm around her waist, she only considered here and now, wisdom be damned.

"The view is stunning," she said as they watched the lights of the marina begin to fade in the distance.

He nuzzled the side of her neck below her ear and whispered, "You are stunning."

She sipped another drink to soothe her parched mouth. "And you, as always, are quick with the compliments."

Suddenly he dropped his arm from around her, prompting her to turn and meet his serious expression. "Never doubt my sincerity when it involves you, Kira. From the first time we met, you have invaded my fantasies on a daily and nightly basis."

She could relate to that, yet some serious issues between them still existed. "This is all a fantasy, too, Tarek. The dress and the dinner and especially the dancing. Tomorrow we'll be back to normal. You're the consummate global businessman on the fast track to continuing success while amassing a fortune. I'm the daughter of domestics who doesn't require all the finer things in life and yearns for a common life with a husband and kids. We are two very different people."

After setting his flute on a nearby cocktail table, he took her glass from her clutches and placed it beside his. He then returned to her and slid his arms back around her, pulling her closer.

"Do you not wish to travel the world before you *settle* into a domestic routine?" He made the word *settle* sound blasphemous.

"I've seen quite a bit of it already. I've also seen sheer happiness in the faces of the Mehdi brothers and their wives. Call me a fool, but I want to experience that, too."

His features went stony again, yet he didn't let her go. "What do you expect from me, Kira?"

To be a father to our baby. To want what I want. To fall desperately in love with me.

The last thought took her mind by surprise and her heart by storm. She didn't want his love. She wanted his respect and willingness to be involved in their child's life. She certainly didn't want to fall in love with him even though at times she thought she could be precariously close to going down that ill-advised path. But not knowing everything about him, and falling into that trap, could be disastrous.

Kira chalked the threatening fuzzy feelings up to a romantic evening with a sexy rogue and pregnancy hormones that had her emotions running amok.

"I don't want anything you're not willing to give, Tarek."

He feathered a kiss across her lips. "I am willing to give you all the pleasure possible. I wish us to be together again in every way. I want you not to concern yourself over the future beyond what we experience tonight. Life is too brief to discard what we have found together."

She rode the waves of confusing emotions. "You're referring to sex."

"I am referring to our undeniable desire for each other. I have never before experienced what I feel with you in my arms. It is very powerful, yet it leaves me powerless. No woman before you has done that."

He seemed bent on saying all the right things. "Not one?"

"No."

"Not even Athena?"

His frown deepened. "Definitely not. And now that she is no longer employed by me, you will not have to endure her again."

A total shock to Kira's already shaky system. "Did you fire her?"

"She resigned, with my blessing."

"Why?"

"She knew she could not compete with you."

Flattery could get him everywhere. Flattery had already immersed her in hot water one other time. She truly, truly didn't care about then, or tomorrow, only now.

On that note, she wrapped one hand around his neck, pulled him to her mouth and kissed him.

Kira soon found herself pressed against the railing, Tarek's hands roving over her bare back as he kissed his way down her neck, pausing to slide his tongue down the valley between her breasts. When he worked his way back up to her lips, he also worked her dress up her thighs and clasped her bare bottom.

He leaned back and grinned. "I believe you forgot something, or perhaps you were prepared for this."

"None of the above. I was trying to avoid unsightly lines."

"I am disappointed it was not the latter."

"Although I wasn't thinking about it at the time, it is very convenient."

His dark gaze bore through any resistance she might

still retain. "I want to touch you, yet I will not do so unless you convince me you want this, too."

She swallowed hard. "Yes, I want this."

"No regrets if we proceed?"

Maybe a few, but she didn't want to consider that now. "No regrets."

"Then show me exactly *where* you want me to touch you."

Kira suddenly felt self-conscious. "Here in wide open spaces?"

"Yes."

Maybe if they were completely alone… "What about Max?"

"He is piloting the boat. He cannot see us unless he decides to drive in reverse back to the port."

True, since they were at the rear of the yacht. But still… "Aren't you just a bit concerned about passing watercraft?"

He briefly kissed her again. "The possibility of discovery only increases the desire. You did say you wanted to be daring."

Kira couldn't believe how often her words had come back to bite her. She also couldn't believe the sudden surge of bravery she experienced at that second. The absolute high she felt when she shifted his hand between her thighs. The unquestionable heat and dampness when he began to stroke gently. For a moment, she felt as though her legs might not hold her, and as if Tarek sensed that, he circled his arm around her waist to provide support.

As the climax began to build, she tipped her forehead

against his chest and let the orgasm take hold, riding it out until every last spasm dissipated. She trembled in the aftermath, even after her respiration and heart rate returned to normal.

Tarek lifted her chin and covered her face with kisses. "You were obviously ready."

No kidding. "Obviously."

"Would you wish to go back inside now?"

Oh, yes. "As long as there is a bed available so we can finish this."

He seemed surprised by the comment. "As long as you are pleased, that is not necessary."

How dare he work her into a sexual frenzy and attempt to leave her high and not exactly dry. "Actually, it is necessary. I want to make love with you again completely."

His expression displayed his pleasure over her declaration. "If you are certain, I would like nothing better."

"I am." And strangely, she was, even knowing that inviting this kind of intimacy probably wasn't wise.

"Then we do not require a bed," he said in a low, deep voice that could convince a middle-aged spinster to hand over her virtue to him.

Kira started to argue that standing against the rail wasn't a banner idea, particularly in her condition, when he clasped her hand and guided her to a sectional sofa covered in blue stripes. He let her go, shrugged out of his jacket and set it aside, all while she awaited further instruction with barely controlled excitement.

"During our last interlude, we failed to use a condom in the heat of passion," he added, his hand poised on his zipper. "Although you did assure me you were protected against pregnancy, would you prefer we use one now to provide peace of mind?"

If she had known what she knew now, she would have insisted on it back then. If he knew what she knew now, this would all be over before it had begun. "I can promise you the pregnancy issue isn't a problem, as long as I can trust you're still okay on the safety front."

"As I told you that night, I have been judicious when it comes to my health. I would never put you in danger."

The conviction in his tone helped ease her concerns. "Then I suppose we should do what comes naturally."

His smile arrived slowly. "Then so we shall."

After he pushed his pants and underwear down to his thighs, he held out both hands. "Come to me."

Shades of the last time they made love. If she'd learned nothing else, she now knew Tarek's preference when it came to positions. She also questioned whether this aided him in avoiding too much intimacy.

Kira kicked off her heels, hiked up her dress, and straddled his lap. She guided him inside her, all the while keeping her gaze leveled on his. She recalled how good this had felt the first time, acknowledged how good he felt now. The guilt monster tried to rear its head, but she beat it down, determined to enjoy this.

She definitely enjoyed watching his face as he clasped her hips while she moved slowly, surely. His efforts at maintaining control showed in the tight set of his jaw and the way his brows furrowed.

Kira wanted him in that powerless state, so she took him deeper and witnessed when his fortress of self-control began to crumble. She was also primed for surrender when he slowed the pace.

"I want this to last," he told her in a harsh whisper. "I refuse to let it end too quickly."

"Are you strong enough to resist, Tarek?" she asked as she wriggled her hips.

"I have always been strong enough. Before you."

Kira had to admit that made her feel somewhat special, and empowered.

They engaged in a sensual war of wills, seeing who would give in first as they shared a smile and soft kisses. She so wished they could be closer, not physically but emotionally. She so wanted to mean more to him than only this. She didn't dare put any stock in that unless she wanted to set herself up for the ultimate disappointment.

A few minutes later, Tarek's respiration grew ragged while moisture beaded his forehead and finally, he closed his eyes. Every muscle in his body seemed to tense beneath her before he bowed his head, signaling his own climax wasn't far way. And then came the low groan followed by a long breath and few crude words muttered in Arabic that she understood well, thanks to being around the Mehdi brothers during her formative years.

He tipped his head back, his eyes still closed. "You win, yet I have never been so happy in losing."

Smiling, Kira laid her cheek against his chest and listened to the steady beat of his heart while he softly rubbed her back. Perhaps making love on a boat deck would be deemed casual and unconventional, but she felt no less in tune with him. She waited for the remorse, for the internal lectures over letting this happen, and actively participating, yet they didn't come. No matter what transpired between them in the days ahead, or if he disappeared from her life for good after learning the truth, she would cherish the memories. And in a perfect world, when their child asked if they ever loved each other, she wished she could honestly say they did. Regretfully, she knew all too well a perfect world didn't exist.

Tarek had never been in love before, and he had no intention of traveling that road. Yet as he watched Kira, curled up beside him on the bed, her hands resting on the pillow beneath her cheek, eyes closed and face slack with sleep, he experienced emotions he had never welcomed, nor felt, until now.

In his life, love had come with betrayal. Betrayed by his mother and the man he had known as his father. Betrayed by a monarch who had denied him. Deep in his soul, he believed Kira to be different. She demanded honesty and he felt as if he could place his faith in her. Yet he also believed he could not offer her a long-term future.

Tomorrow morning, his first order of business for the day involved a request that would allow them more time together for however long they had left. If all went as planned, she would assist him in overseeing the completion of the resort. He would gladly offer her an opportunity to expand her expertise, even if he could not offer her more, provided she did not refuse him.

Seven

"That's impossible." And unrealistic for Tarek to assume she could extend her time in Cyprus and ignore her responsibilities to the royal family.

He scooted up against the headboard, giving Kira a bird's-eye view of his bare chest, which didn't help her concentration. "You would only be required to remain for another week to ten days," he said.

She pulled the covers up to her neck and sighed. "Rafiq would never agree to that."

"He already has."

She rolled to her side, her mouth agape. "You asked him before you asked me?"

"Yes. I had to make certain I had his permission before I spoke with you. He claims that Miss Battelli is thoroughly enjoying resuming her duties for the time being."

Elena would never let on if she wasn't. Then again, Kira might be out of a job when she returned. "At any rate, it's not fair to her to interrupt her well-deserved retirement just so I can continue to frolic about with you for another two weeks."

"I do not frolic."

She had inadvertently trampled on his manhood. "You know what I mean, so don't get your ego in a tangle."

He shifted to his side and extracted her grip from the gold Egyptian cotton sheet. "You would gain great experience overseeing the project." He rolled her hand over and kissed her wrist. "You would gain great pleasure spending more nights with me."

The memories of their lovemaking, both on the deck and in the bed at dawn, fogged her already hazy mind. The boat hadn't been the only thing rocking last night. "I don't have the experience Athena has."

"Perhaps, yet your talents are more far reaching than Athena's." He slid his palm across her belly, causing her to shiver slightly. "That does not include only your business acumen."

She should push that wicked hand away, but she didn't want to. "You're not playing fair."

He stroked the inside of her thigh with his knuckles. "You were not complaining about fairness this morning when I woke you."

No. She had mostly been moaning. "You're insatiable."

"You are responsible for that," he said as he made his way to his favorite target.

If he kept touching her, she couldn't be responsible for anything she might do next. "If we're going to get some significant work done today, we're going to have to get out of the bed at some point in time."

"Eventually." He nuzzled his face against her shoulder. "It is still early."

Kira glanced toward the nightstand to search for a clock but instead found a picture of a little girl who looked to be around five years old. She reached for the frame and turned it toward him. "Who is this?"

He immediately removed his hand and shifted to his back, one arm lodged behind his head. "Her name is Yasmin."

"Is she a relative's child?"

"She is no one's child."

This was both sad and confusing to Kira. "I don't understand."

"She is an orphan in Morocco. I learned about her from a business associate and agreed to be her guardian. She resides at my home in Marrakech."

Only one more surprising aspect of Tarek Azzmar's life. "I assume she doesn't live there alone."

"Of course not. I have a well-qualified French au pair and a very accommodating staff."

And a well-kept secret. "Why have you never mentioned her before?"

"As I have said, I prefer to maintain a certain standard of privacy."

The understatement of the century. "What is your role in her care, Tarek? Do you have an attachment to her, or are you only her benefactor?"

"I am very fond of Yasmin. I place a call to her every evening."

One mystery solved. "But you don't care enough to be a real father to her."

He flashed a look of anger before he left the bed to put on the robe draped on the chrome footboard. He then crossed to the window to stare out at the view, keeping his back to her. "This is why I did not mention Yasmin to you, or to anyone, for that matter. I assumed people would not understand, and clearly I have been correct in those assumptions."

Oh, but she did understand. Much more than he realized. The time had come to go quid pro quo and share a part of her past. First, she sat up and pulled her knees to her chest, taking care to remain completely covered. "I understand what it's like to be abandoned, Tarek."

The painful admission sent him around to face her. "Are you referring to your ex-fiancé?"

"I'm referring to my biological parents. I'm adopted. My mother couldn't have children."

He returned to the bed and perched on the mattress. "Obviously I have not been the only one withholding information."

If he only knew what she still withheld from him. But this newfound knowledge could be a good lead-in to telling him about the baby. "I personally haven't mentioned it to very many people because I consider my adoptive parents my real parents. They've been the greatest positive influence on me."

He sent her a fast glance before returning his attention to some unknown focal point across the yacht's cabin. "Do you know your biological parents' identities?"

"Yes. They were both Canadian and fifteen years old when I was born. Like Yasmin, I came to them through a personal connection. My parents were friends with a relative of my biological grandmother, who happens to be an attorney. She assisted in the arrangements for a private adoption."

He finally shifted so she could see his face. "Have you had contact with your birth mother?"

She shook her head. "No. It was a closed adoption, although I did locate my birth mother a few years back. She declined speaking with me by phone or in person because apparently she hadn't told her current husband and children that I even existed. She did send an email though."

The fury returned to his features. "Does this not anger you, knowing you have siblings you have never met and a mother who cared so little about knowing you?"

Disappointed would be much more accurate. "Actually, it did bother me a bit at first, but I respect her decision to maintain her privacy. I also called off the search for my birth father."

"Why?"

"Because I saw no use in bothering him when it's probable he doesn't want to be located, either. Besides, I grew up in a loving home with two wonderful, encouraging people. I came to the conclusion that those responsible for my birth played a very small role in who I am today. My mama and papa are completely responsible for giving me the foundation I needed to succeed, and that's all that matters."

Tarek pushed off the bed and began to pace. "I would be enraged if I were you. Everyone has the right to learn about those who have brought them into this world."

She was taken aback by the strength of his animosity. "Getting angry gets you nowhere, Tarek. You couldn't begin to understand unless you've been there."

He spun toward her. "Anger can be a motivator to succeed."

"Not in this case. Anger only makes you bitter if you remain rooted in past recriminations." She suddenly realized they'd gone completely off topic in terms of the little girl. "Now back to Yasmin. Apparently you have fond feelings for her or you wouldn't have a photo at your bedside."

"Yes, I care for her, but my time is limited due to my career. That is why I have carefully chosen people who can give her what I cannot."

Kira found his apathy discouraging. "You mean all you have to offer is money? Anyone can provide monetarily for a child, but nurturing is more important."

"She receives ample attention."

He didn't quite get it, and possibly never would. "But does she have enough emotional support? You may think you've saved her from a life of loneliness, but if she is attached to you in any way, then you are not saving her from anything every time you leave her behind."

He returned to the edge of the bed and ran both hands through his ruffled dark hair. "It is the only way at this time."

"Then why did you take her in?"

"She was a child in need. An innocent without a family."

Kira was slowly coming to the conclusion that perhaps he wasn't cut out for fatherhood. "I hope that you'll think about spending more time with her while she's still young. She needs a father, not a stranger looking after her."

He abruptly stood and headed toward the en suite bath. "We must ready for the day since it is growing late."

Kira worried it might be too late for Tarek to change.

Upon arrival at the resort, Tarek dove into the activity that normally gave him the most solace. Yet as he cut the stone for the wall, his mind kept turning to his conversation with Kira that morning. He had not been able to express how much Yasmin meant to him. Each time he left the child, he had to steel his heart in order not to stay with her. Perhaps he had done a disservice by taking her in. Perhaps he was still doing that by keeping her. Still, he could not fathom giving her away after two years.

For the first time in quite a while, someone had forced him to take a hard look at his choices. That same someone had caused him to question his decisions on several levels. Kira Darzin remained unaware of how much she had affected him in ways he had not anticipated.

"Looks like you're almost finished with that."

Tarek peered up from his handiwork to find the

woman who constantly invaded this thoughts and dreams standing nearby. "I still have much to do to make certain it is perfect."

Kira dropped onto a nearby bench and adjusted the hem of her aqua dress to her knees, as if she had been overcome with modesty. "At times, the beauty is in the imperfections."

He considered her absolute perfection, especially her haunting cobalt eyes that looked much lighter reflecting the noon sun. "Perhaps, but I am at times a perfectionist."

She gave the impression she was quite skeptical. "Only at times?"

"The majority of the time, if you must know."

"That's what I thought." She cleared her throat and briefly looked away. "I wanted to apologize to you about our conversation this morning. I didn't give you enough credit. Providing Yasmin with a safe place to stay is very magnanimous."

Yet she had inadvertently pointed out an obvious flaw in his character. "There is no need for that."

"Yes, there is. I have no right to judge you. Many men wouldn't give an orphan a second thought, much less open their homes to one. They would rather give money and let someone else handle it. You should be commended for your compassion."

He tossed aside the trowel and leaned a hip against the work table. "Save your commendation for someone who merits it. You were correct on several points. Yasmin does need a full-time father figure. She needs a man who deserves to be called papa."

"Is that what she calls you?" Kira asked, a note of awe in her voice.

"Yes."

"Then apparently that's how she sees you."

"It makes me somewhat uncomfortable," he reluctantly admitted.

"Why?"

"Because I believe I am not worthy of the endearment."

"Maybe you should work a little harder to remedy that."

She would not understand his reticence unless he explained further. "I fear she will become too attached to me."

Kira's frown deepened. "I don't view that as a problem unless you plan to send her away."

"I would never consider such a thing." His tone sounded unquestionably defensive.

She studied him for awhile as if trying to peer into his very soul. "Then maybe you're afraid you're going to become too attached to her."

Her insight astounded him. "Perhaps you are correct."

She crossed one leg over the other and leveled her gaze on his, as if preparing to analyze him. "What's the basis for this fear, Tarek?"

"Attachment leads to betrayal. You should know that as well in regard to your former fiancé." Now he had said too much.

She swept one hand through her hair as she appeared to ponder that a time. "That's different, Tarek. We're talking about a child. I'm going to guess that your parents somehow wronged you, or maybe you feel betrayed by your mother's death."

He had been deceived by his mother, yet not in the way Kira believed.

When a landscaper began planting shrubs nearby, Tarek thought it best to suspend the conversation. "Our privacy has now been disturbed so it is better we return to our duties. Did the table you requested for the kitchen arrive?"

Kira rose from the bench and sent him a slight smile. "Yes, and it's exactly what I was looking for. I'm about to meet with the designer and inspect the furniture in the restaurant. Would you like to go with me and give your seal of approval?"

He would like to go with her to another place that had nothing to do with the resort. "I plan to complete this project before day's end."

She did not appear at all pleased with that. "I hope you return to the villa tonight at a decent hour so we can finish this discussion."

As far as he was concerned, they had. "I should be there before sundown, yet I would prefer to spend our evening in ways that will not require discourse."

She started away before hesitating and facing him again. "It's really imperative we talk, Tarek. I have something important I need to tell you."

He could only imagine what that might be. Perhaps in her eyes he now seemed dishonorable due to his reluctance to permanently commit to raising Yasmin. Or perhaps she no longer intended to stay. Regardless, he would attempt to convince her that he wanted her by his side, for however much time they still had together. He had the means, and the methods, to make her forget they ever had this conversation, though he most likely never would forget.

The man was nowhere to be found. Avoidance, plain and simple.

Kira strode through the living area in search of someone who could tell her Tarek's whereabouts. She assumed their conversation earlier today had him running scared. Or at least running from her.

She reached the cook's kitchen—all stainless steel, granite and glass—to find the one member of the staff who seemed to have a human radar where his employer was concerned. "Alexios," she began, "have you seen Mr. Azzmar? He didn't come back for dinner and I was wonder—"

"He's taking a walk on the shoreline, Ms. Darzin," he replied without missing a beat folding the cloth napkins. "He told me to inform you of his location should you need to speak with him."

Oh, she needed to speak with him all right. And he knew it. "Thank you for another wonderful dinner tonight." Too bad she'd had to spend it alone. Again.

Kira made her way past the pool and through the gate that led to the private beach. The moon wasn't quite as full as it had been on their impromptu cruise, but it provided enough light to guide her way. She didn't have to walk far to see the silhouette of a man seated in the sand, his arms casually resting on bent knees.

After kicking off her sandals near a small rock formation, Kira approached him slowly and the closer she came, the better she could see his profile. *Handsome and rich*, her first thought. *Troubled and stoic*, her second. He seemed so immersed in contemplation, she almost hated to disturb him. But the mission she was on—sharing the information that might very well change their future—could no longer keep. She'd waited too long to tell him and worried that he wouldn't take the news well, even though she'd seen a nurturing side to him that both pleased and surprised her.

In a matter of minutes, she arrived at his side, claimed the spot beside him and hugged her legs to her chest. "You look rather pensive tonight."

"I have been reflecting on what you said to me this morning about Yasmin."

She regretted some of her comments, but others, not so much. "I didn't mean to intrude, Tarek."

His thoughts seemed to drift away momentarily before he began to speak again. "She is a very gregarious little girl. She possesses a free spirit and rarely goes anywhere without running." He paused to smile. "She is also quite the conversationalist. At times, I listen quietly to her only to hear the sound of her voice. She seems unaffected by the hardship that has befallen her."

The hint of emotion in his voice touched Kira deeply. "Children are resilient. They only want to be loved."

His expression turned suddenly somber. "Perhaps another family would better serve her needs, one with both a mother and father."

We could have that family, she wanted to say, but

stopped short of spilling her secret. "You don't give yourself enough credit, Tarek. You have inherent compassion and the capacity to love her more than you realize."

He glanced at her, then reached over and took her hand. "I sincerely appreciate your faith in me, yet I feel as if I am bereft of any true emotion. I am not certain I can change that."

She leaned her head against his shoulder. "Hearing you talk so fondly about Yasmin leads me to believe you already have. Or maybe those emotions have always been there and you're simply afraid to feel them. I'm really sorry that someone has hurt you that badly."

He remained silent as he rubbed his thumb back and forth over her wrist in a soothing rhythm. "It is warm tonight."

Leave it to him to talk about the weather when she was getting too close for his comfort. "It's a beautiful night. Just enough breeze to make it totally comfortable."

Without warning, he leaned back and took her with him. Without words, he kissed her thoroughly. She so needed to ask him to stop so she could tell him about their child. She also needed to protest when he rolled her onto her back and slid his hand beneath her top to cup her silk-covered breasts.

"Tarek, we still need to talk," she managed when he turned his attention to her neck.

"Later," he muttered as he brushed his knuckles down her belly.

Later seemed like a banner idea, especially when he

released the button below her waist and slid her zipper down. Much later, she decided as he worked the cotton shorts down her hips, taking her panties with them. She didn't have the strength to utter one protest when he moved over her, gently parted her thighs and kissed his way down her torso.

Now there she was, lying on a bed of sand, completely out in the open with her bottoms down to her ankles and Tarek working his magic with his talented mouth between her legs. The ultimate intimacy could prove to be her emotional and physical undoing. The tempered strokes of his tongue could send her straight to the three-quarter moon above them. The ensuing climax could very well cause her to actually scream from the pleasure.

Fortunately she had enough presence of mind to remain quiet except for a low moan when the orgasm took over. She couldn't recall ever feeling so grand and so ready for Tarek to complete this sensual journey.

She had to wait for him to shrug out of his white tailored shirt, which he spread out on the ground.

"Lay on this," he said as he took off his slacks and underwear.

As Kira stretched out on the makeshift blanket, Tarek joined her and guided himself inside her. He kept his gaze locked on hers while he moved lightly at first, as if bent on teasing her into oblivion.

She loved the closeness of his body, the feel of his weight. She loved the sound of his breath at her ear, growing more uneven with each passing second. She loved the power of his thrusts, the crude but sexy words he uttered until he didn't speak at all. She loved…him. She had no idea when it had happened, or why she would let herself be so vulnerable. She did know that despite his efforts to present himself as a man who wanted no emotional ties, a caring man resided beneath the hardnosed businessman.

After Tarek collapsed against her, Kira stroked his back and relished the feel of his weight. All too soon, he rolled over and draped an arm over his eyes. They lay there for quite some time beneath a host of stars, serenaded by the sound of lapping waves. She could stay here forever, shutting out everything aside from these few special moments. But the secret she held— the one she desperately needed to tell him—continued to play over and over in her mind.

Tarek transferred back to his side, rose above her on one elbow and smiled. "You are a most amazing woman."

She released a curt laugh. "First the boat, now the beach. I'm beginning to think I'm an exhibitionist."

"You are more daring than you would wish to believe."

Yet not quite daring enough to blurt out the truth. "I've never been that way before you. Actually, you're only the second man I've been with."

He looked both pleased and surprised. "I am honored. You are the first woman I have trusted implicitly."

The gravity of what she had to reveal weighed heavily on her heart. If she told him now, she would ruin the wonderful aftermath of their lovemaking. And when he kissed her tenderly again, she decided to wait until tomorrow to tell him she had been lying to him all along. With that revelation came the probability of a permanent goodbye.

Eight

"Have you not told him yet, *cara mia*?"

Seated cross-legged in the middle of Tarek's king-size bed, Kira gripped the cell phone and instantly regretted calling Elena to check on the state of affairs at the palace. "No, I haven't found the right time."

"You have been there almost three weeks."

She found herself caught in the grip of shame. "Yes, but we've been very busy readying the resort. The grand opening is less than a month away."

"And I would estimate your pregnancy should begin to show around that time."

Kira realized Elena was right. Her waistbands had already begun to grow tighter and her belly had become much more rounded. If Tarek had noticed, he hadn't said. He'd definitely seen her eat like two-hundred-pound man, and naked on more than one occasion. "The signs aren't obvious unless you know I'm pregnant. And I promise I'm going to tell him very soon. At least before I return to Bajul next week."

"I believe it is imperative you do and soon. Now I have a question for you. Do you happen to know Tarek's mother's first name?"

"Actually, no, I don't. Why?"

"Someone I once knew a long time ago was acquainted with a woman by the last name of Azzmar."

"Was she from Morocco?"

"Yes."

"That's odd. I'd wager the chances of it being the same woman are slim, but it is a small world."

"Much smaller than you realize, *cara*. Please call me when you are on your way to Bajul. And if you don't mind, ask Tarek to stop by and see me when he returns to the palace. Perhaps we can make a connection between the two women."

That seemed like a strange request. "I'll ask him, but I make no promises. He's very guarded about his parents."

"I have no doubt about that. Stay well, Kira."

With that, the line went dead, and Kira's mind shot into overdrive. Elena's cryptic words could keep her guessing for the duration of her stay in Cyprus. Tarek's astounding lovemaking could keep her in a sexual frenzy as well.

As if she'd conjured him up, the breathtaking billionaire strolled into the room wearing a black shirt and tan slacks, along with a sinfully sexy look. "It is nice to have the remainder of the day off."

It was nice to see him after spending the morning with a cross contractor who didn't care for her suggestions. "We deserve it after working so hard the past few weeks." Busy weeks dealing with the resort pitfalls and wonderful nights spent in the throes of passion.

Hands in pockets, he approached the bed slowly. "How would you propose we spend the time today?"

Playing truth or consequences per her promise to Elena would be good. Kira patted the space beside her and geared up for the revelation she had put off for too long. "We could talk for a few minutes." *Or not*, she thought, as Tarek toed out of his loafers, pulled off his socks and began unbuttoning his shirt.

After he removed and kicked off his slacks and underwear, he stood beside the bed looking like a very proud Adonis. "We will talk later," he said as he crawled toward her like a sexy, stalking cougar. "At this moment, I need you very badly."

"I noticed." Boy, had she ever.

He rose to his knees, quickly divested her of the yellow sundress that didn't require a bra, slid her panties down to toss them over his shoulder and then gave her a long, lingering look. "I wish to have you this way all the time."

"That might be awkward when we're out in public."

He smiled as he circled her nipple with a fingertip. "Would you like to try something new?"

She managed to move the comforter from beneath her and Tarek, uncovering another set of exquisite silver sheets. "Are you suggesting perhaps we make love on the rooftop? We've already initiated your shower, this bed several times, the beach, the yacht, and oh yes, the supply closet at the resort. Lucky for us we didn't get caught."

He sent her a knockout grin before he kissed her senseless, using his wicked tongue in some very suggestive ways. "I suppose we could utilize the kitchen countertops here," he began after breaking the kiss, "but unfortunately dinner preparation has begun."

She wrapped her arms around his neck and smiled at his sudden show of humor. "Honestly, I like being on a comfy mattress."

"I was actually suggesting a new position we have not tried before." He rolled her to her side and whispered, "One that will only enhance your climax."

When he pressed his erection against her bottom, she looked back with him over one shoulder. "I'm going to trust you on this."

He draped her leg over his thigh. "You may trust that you will feel sensations you have never felt before."

When Tarek slipped inside her, Kira wholeheartedly agreed with his assessment. She keenly experienced every nuance of his body as he began to move in a steady rhythm, felt every gentle caress with heightened awareness as he delved between her legs with skilled fingers. She did miss seeing his face so she could witness that instant when he achieved his release, but his nearness almost made up for that piece of the sensual Tarek puzzle.

When he picked up the tempo, with both his thrusts

and touches, Kira quit thinking about anything as her orgasm began to arrive with the speed of a runaway locomotive. The first strong spasm hit, but Tarek didn't let up, bringing their lovemaking to new, wild heights. She felt the tension in his frame and heard the sound of his harsh breathing as he tightened his hold on her. By the time he climaxed with a shudder and a groan, Kira was as spent as she'd ever been in his arms, and more satisfied than she ever thought possible.

In the quiet aftermath, she realized all too well that this would soon be coming to an end, something she had known all along but hadn't wanted to accept. Even if Tarek opted to be a part of his child's life, he would never forgive her for not telling him sooner. He would probably want nothing to do with her after they left Cyprus. Only one way to find out, as painful as it might be.

After Tarek laid back and took her into his arms, Kira rested her cheek on his chest, her favorite place to be. A brief span of silence passed before she decided it might be best to lead into the disclosure with casual conversation. "I talked with Elena right before you came in."

He began rubbing the side of her thigh with slow, even strokes, refueling her hormones and hindering her concentration. "I hope all is well with the palace and you are not being summoned back to Bajul."

"Everything's fine," she said as she listened to the steady beat of his heart. "I do have a message for you from Elena, though. She wants you to stop by when we're back in Bajul and meet with her."

"For what reason?"

"Something about a Moroccan woman with your last name that a friend of hers once knew. She thinks you might have a mutual connection."

He suddenly stopped caressing her altogether. "I would be surprised if that were the case. There are several Moroccan citizens with my surname."

"That's what I told her, but I promised I'd pass the message on to you."

"I will see her if I can find the time when I return." His tone sounded strangely irritable, as if he found the request unpalatable. She couldn't imagine anyone not liking the former governess. Nevertheless, a subject change seemed to be in order. One that would aid in the transition to baby news.

"Have you spoken with Yasmin lately?" she asked.

"Earlier this morning," he said. "She is very pleased over the puppy I gave her, though he is a mixed breed that one of my staff found wandering the streets."

"Those are the best kind of dogs."

"Yasmin seems to believe that to be the case. She called to tell me she has named him after me."

He had given a child a dog, and that indicated he had good paternal instincts. The fact that the child had given the dog his name spoke to her fondness for her reluctant replacement patriarch. "I'm sure there aren't too many Tareks running around in the canine world."

"Not Tarek. She calls him Poppy, which she has called me when she's attempting to persuade me into allowing her to have a treat or stay up past her bedtime."

Just a few more indicators that he must be closer to

the little girl than he'd previously led on. "Sounds to me like she's quite smitten with you, too."

"She is a good-natured child."

She could be his real child if he'd only give fatherhood a chance. Maybe knowing he would soon have a baby of his own would prompt him to change his mind.

The time had come to make the announcement, and face the inevitable.

In an effort to get down to serious business, something she couldn't do while naked, Kira sat up and covered herself with the rumpled sheet, bringing about Tarek's groan of protest. If she only knew how to begin without blurting, "I'm pregnant." A plan started to form, one that involved guiding him into the information minefield without tossing a verbal grenade.

She grabbed a pillow from behind her and put it in a choke hold. "Have you considered maybe getting a playmate for Yasmin?"

He scowled. "A pet does not qualify?"

"I meant a human playmate. A brother or a sister. I grew up as an only child and know firsthand how lonely that can be, although I did have the good fortune to have the Mehdis as surrogate brothers."

He frowned. "I also grew up as an only child and I fared well. Since Yasmin is not officially my offspring, giving her a sibling would be impossible. You have also pointed out I do not carve out enough time for her. If I took in another orphan, I would be depriving them both."

Time to test the paternity waters. "Perhaps you

should consider finding someone special to share the child-rearing responsibility."

"As I have stated before, I have an exceptional au pair."

Could he be more obtuse? "*Special* as in a spouse. Since you're a couple of years away from forty, don't you think it's time to consider settling down? If you're like most men I know, surely you'd like to have a son who can inherit your fortune and carry on your legacy."

"I have that option with Yasmin."

"Yet you haven't made a move to adopt her and give her your name, although I sense you truly care about her. What makes you steer clear of anyone who gets too close to you?"

He pushed off the bed and began to pace. "Love comes with conditions and, many times, lies."

Kira clutched the covers tighter in her fists as her anxiety increased. "Who lied to you, Tarek? Another woman? Athena? Believe me, I know what it's like to be betrayed by a lover. But it's important to move on and not let that experience guide your choices and keep you closed off to all the possibilities."

He stopped and streaked a hand over his nape. "This has nothing to do with a lover, and it does not matter now. I prefer to leave the past in the past."

Stubborn, stubborn man. "That sounds good, but I don't think you're doing that at all."

"You do not know all there is to know about me, Kira."

"And you don't know all about me either, Tarek. Honestly, I've tried to tell you several times since we've been here, but you somehow always manage to distract me." She sighed. "Or maybe I thought if I avoided revealing everything it would somehow all go away. But this is not going to go away."

After slipping his pants back on, Tarek moved to the end of the bed and braced his palms on the footboard. "Are you wed to someone else?"

She found that almost laughable in the midst of a humorless situation. "Of course not."

"You have a secret lover?"

"No. Not even close."

"You have a secret child?"

"You're definitely getting warmer." And from the stern look on his face, she was poised to walk right into the fire.

"No more guessing games, Kira. Tell me what you have been keeping from me."

"I'm pregnant with your baby." There, she'd said it, and the sky hadn't fallen. Tarek's expression did, right before recognition dawned.

"How long have you known this?" he asked, his tone teeming with anger.

She'd dreaded this part most of all. "I confirmed it at the doctor's appointment on the day you asked me to come to Cyprus with you. That was part of the reason I agreed to make the trip."

"Yet you did not afford me the courtesy of telling me the news before we left."

The indictment in his tone made Kira shiver. "I wanted to get to know you better and try to find out how you would react. It's fairly apparent you are not happy about it."

He laced his hands behind his head and turned his back on her. "You assured me you were protected against pregnancy. Was that a lie as well?"

Her own anger reached the boiling point. "If you think for a minute I trapped you by intentionally getting pregnant, think again. When I heard the news, at first I was devastated, then confused. But once I became accustomed to the idea, I decided I am going to have this baby and love it and care for it whether you come along for the ride or not."

Without responding, Tarek began to put on the rest of his clothes. Kira wrapped up in the sheet and climbed out of the bed, intent on forcing him to express his feelings. "Don't you have anything else you want to say to me, Tarek?"

"I need to think," he said as he headed out the bedroom door.

On the verge of tears, Kira resigned herself to the fact that her biggest fear had been realized—Tarek Azzmar had no intention of being a father.

He had intended to return to the resort, yet several hours later, he found himself driving a newly purchased Porsche along the coastline with no definitive destination. Kira's declaration continued to occupy his thoughts as he turned back in the direction of the villa.

I'm pregnant with your baby...

Not once had a woman ever uttered those words to

him, even as an empty threat. Not once had he believed he would hear them spoken as the truth.

In spite of his ongoing shock, he needed to talk with her soon, even if he could not say what she needed to hear. Granted, he did have feelings for her more powerful than any he had ever experienced with any woman. Perhaps with any living soul, aside from Yasmin. Yet Kira deserved better than a bitter, broken man bent on revenge, and so did his unborn child as well as Yasmin. If he could not devote all his time to his charges, or be the kind of father Mika'il Azzmar had been to him, he would be doing his offspring a disservice.

As soon as he returned to the villa, Tarek handed over the car to a confused Alexios and entered the house to look for Kira. After a brief search, he found her seated at the bistro table on the terrace outside the master bedroom, the favored place where they had shared several intimate conversations and sexual interludes. Unfortunately, those late-night discussions had not included information he should have been privy to weeks ago. Logically, he could not fault her for the concealment since he, too, had been withholding his own secrets, yet he could not deny his continued anger over yet another betrayal.

The lies would soon come to an end.

Tarek strode through the open doors and claimed the chair opposite Kira, who seemed taken aback by his appearance. They sat in silence for a time, avoiding each other's gazes until Kira cleared her throat.

"Are you calm enough to talk reasonably now?" she asked.

Externally calm, yes, but not internally. "I am as calm as humanly possible under the circumstances."

She sipped water from a glass clutched in her delicate hand. "Look, neither of us expected this, but how we feel no longer involves only us. We have to decide how we're going to proceed for the baby's sake."

He would need more time to adjust to the reality of a child. "Rest assured, I will make certain you and the child will be more than adequately compensated. Aside from that, I have little to say at this point in time in light of your lack of warning." And one more betrayal in a long line of many.

She looked as distressed as he felt. "I wish I would have told you sooner, Tarek, but I didn't know how. Regardless, this is *our* child, Tarek, and I don't want your money. In fact, I don't need it. I'd rather be struggling and loved than rich and lonely."

He would endeavor to set her straight. "Wealth does not equal loneliness, Kira."

"Sure, if you don't mind buying friends."

She had touched a nerve with her veiled accusation, causing his anger to return with the force of a hurricane. "You have no right to judge my character after what you have withheld from me.."

She leaned forward and centered her gaze on his. "But isn't that exactly what you've done with the Mehdis, isn't it?"

"I consider them business associates as well as acquaintances."

"You've said several things that have led me to believe you hold them in disdain and that definitely includes their father. Of course, that didn't stop you from investing in their conservation project just so you could ingratiate yourself in the family. You even built your mansion in the shadow of the palace. I'm beginning to wonder if this is some sort of contest to see if you can outdo the royals who apparently have something you want."

If she only knew his real reasons for those actions and exactly what he did want from them—acknowledgment that he existed. "You may think what you will, but the project was a sound investment. The estate was an afterthought."

"A nice addition to your collection of estates, I'm sure," she said, her tone heavy with sarcasm. "And it's so ironic that the place is so large, yet you have no one to fill all those empty rooms. Why is that, Tarek?"

At one time he believed the size of one's home determined societal status. Now he was not as certain as he had been in the past. "I spent my formative years in a two-room bungalow where I slept on a cot in the living area. Perhaps that explains my obsession." At one time, he'd believed the size of one's home determined societal status. Now he was not as certain.

"Perhaps, deep down in a place you won't acknowledge, you hope to fill those rooms with family. Then again, that's probably wishful thinking on my part."

He had no desire to debate that theory, yet he needed to force her to understand their dire straits. "You have no idea what the implications of this pregnancy will be."

She took another drink of water, then pushed the glass aside. "If you're worried about losing your standing in the good old boys' rich club, don't. The Mehdis don't have to know you're my baby's father. I, on the other hand, have to worry about possibly losing my position and telling my parents their unwed daughter is expecting their first grandchild. But I know in my heart the royal family and my family will forgive me, whatever the future holds."

To think she would suffer the consequences of their actions troubled him, despite his anger. So did their child's true legacy.

"Again, I will make certain you will want for nothing."

She sat back and released a frustrated sigh. "Okay, Tarek. Toss me a few of your precious dollars every month and maybe set up a college fund for the kid, if that clears your conscience. But one day down the road, when our child grows up, he or she will begin to wonder about his or her father and why he abandoned them. I know that to be true because I wondered the same thing, even if I pretend it doesn't bother me."

Unbeknownst to her, he had felt the same way about his legacy. He still did, and the time had come to state the facts. "There is something you are unaware of regarding my heritage."

Her frown heralded her confusion. "You were born to common folk like me. What else is there to know?"

"I was born to a common mother, but I cannot say the same about my father."

"I thought you said he was a stone mason."

"I am referring to my birth father."

Her expression now showed her shock. "Are you saying the man you grew up with isn't your father?"

"No, he is not. He wed my mother when she was pregnant with me after my biological father abandoned both of us and never acknowledged my existence."

"Where is he now?"

"Dead. I might celebrate that fact, but unfortunately he took to the grave all the information I require about the circumstances that led up to my birth."

She sent him a sympathetic look that he did not want or need. "I'm truly sorry, Tarek, but maybe it's better you don't know the details."

"I demand to know the truth."

She released a weary sigh. "Well, I would like to know the name of this mystery man who's filled you with so much hatred."

For the first time in his life, Tarek would unveil the identity of the tyrant responsible for his abandonment. The bastard who had ignored his own son. The royal leader who had led everyone astray. "Aadil Mehdi, your revered former king of Bajul."

Nine

As her mind began to reel, Kira's shock came out in an audible gasp. Any response escaped her at the moment, then suddenly reality hit home. "This baby is a Mehdi?"

"That appears to be the case," Tarek began, "though I would prefer it not be true. Nothing good can come out of being born into a family of scheming royals who do not know the first thing about earning a living."

Her loyalty to the royal family swiftly kicked in. "The Mehdi brothers are good men, Tarek, and their father was a strong, generous leader."

"He was an autocrat who ignored his country's poor."

Kira had acknowledged long ago the former king wasn't without faults or failures. "It's true he didn't make enough assistance available for them, but Rafiq, Zain and Adan have made great strides in that regard.

Evidently you're too bitter over their father's actions to realize that."

"We will see their true character when I inform them I am the illegitimate son of their former king."

That definitely did not sit well with her in light of her own situation. "Every child is legitimate, Tarek. I despise that label."

"Despise it or not, it still exists and many would see me that way."

She had so many more unanswered questions yet didn't quite know where to begin. "Exactly how did you discover this information?"

A hint of sorrow showed in his dark eyes, but the anger soon returned. "My presumed father told me right before he died. He forced me to swear that I would never reveal my true parentage to honor my mother's memory. Since that day, I have worked tirelessly to prove that in spite of the fact I was shunned and denied my birthright, I am as good as any prince."

That explained his obsessive drive when it came to getting ahead in the business world. "Are you going to tell them you're their half brother?"

"When I deem the time is right."

She didn't have the energy to ask what he meant by that, but she did see a problem with his plan. "If Rafiq, Zain and Adan knew the truth when you'd first met them, they would have probably welcomed you with open arms. But I can't guarantee they'll accept your subterfuge now."

"It is immaterial what they think of me. I do not need their approval."

Sometimes she believed she knew him better than he knew himself. Time to give him a hard lesson on self-awareness. "Their approval is *exactly* what you desire. You all but admitted it a minute ago. And I hope you tell them sooner than later, and that you have proof to back up your claims aside from a dying man's declaration."

"Not presently, yet I am sure someone in the palace is privy to my mother's affair and her lover's abandonment."

She had another disturbing epiphany. "Is that why you sought me out and established a relationship? Have I been some pawn in your ploy to gain information?"

His hesitation spoke volumes. "I would be disingenuous if I said the thought did not cross my mind. Yet when you continually demonstrated your loyalty to the Mehdis, I determined you would not be forthcoming with confidential details."

That gave her very little comfort. "I'm beginning to wonder if your relationship with me has been founded on revenge. What better way to get back at the family you believe wronged you than by seducing a woman who is like a sister to them?"

"I assure you that is not the case. When we met, I was not aware that you grew up with the Mehdis. Aside from that, I would not be surprised if one of the Mehdi sons is aware of my identity."

Kira shook her head. "I don't believe that for a second." She wasn't sure she could believe Tarek on any point. "They would have confronted you the moment you entered their house. In fact, they probably know nothing about your mother's involvement with their father, if it is the truth."

"Or perhaps they are attempting to avoid another scandal."

The palace had been plagued with scandal in recent times, including the revelation that Elena was Adan's biological mother and the former king's longtime lover—a fact that was still kept undercover for the most part—as well as the current king marrying a divorcée. But in comparison, this one could trump them all.

When Kira recalled Elena's peculiar questions regarding Tarek's mother, the mental light switched on. She didn't necessarily like aiding him in the cause, but she had to consider her own child's legacy. "I know who you need to ask about your mother's possible affair with the king."

"If you are suggesting I speak with one of the princes, I would prefer not to begin there."

"No. I'm suggesting you talk to their former governess. She served as the king's confidant for many years. If you're seeking proof, she'll have it if it exists. If it doesn't, what then?"

He rubbed his chin. "I will decide that after I speak with the king's former mistress."

Apparently the continuing secret hadn't been concealed as well as she'd assumed. "How did you find out about that?"

"Adan informed me that Elena is his natural mother and of the circumstances behind his birth. Obviously Aadil could not be loyal to one woman."

She despised the disdain in his voice, particularly

since he didn't know all the pertinent details. "Elena told me their relationship evolved after the queen's death. Her agreement to have Adan when the queen could no longer conceive was only that, an agreement. They never meant for the relationship to blossom the way it did. I do know they loved each other deeply."

"Another love built on lies."

Kira saw no end to his cynicism, and that made her sad. Still, she had one more thing to get off her chest, not that it would make a measurable difference. "Tarek, I love you, although believe me, that's been quite a challenge. I think I fell in love with you the day we took a walk in the garden and you told me about your years at the university and how hard you worked to succeed. You took my hand to make sure I didn't stumble over a stone, and I thought, now there's a true gentleman. But I refuse to stay involved with a man who is so steeped in resentment he no longer appreciates the value in loving someone unconditionally. My baby deserves more and so do I."

She paused to draw a breath. "Yes, I betrayed you by not being honest about the baby from the beginning, and you did the same by not telling me about your suspicions. But every time you cut yourself off from feeling any emotions other than rage, you're betraying yourself. Your baby needs a father who's not afraid to feel something other than anger."

He seemed to mull that over for a time before speaking again. "If I do discover that I am a true son of the king, perhaps it would be best if we wed to give our child a name."

Where had that come from? "Oh, sure, Tarek. Let's engage in that archaic practice of marrying for the sake of a child. Thanks, but no thanks. I would rather raise our baby on my own than be tied to a man who hasn't the first clue how to love someone unconditionally."

When Kira pushed back from the table and came to her feet, Tarek asked, "Where are you going?"

"To my room to pack." And probably cry. "You told me I could decide when to leave, so I plan to do that tomorrow. The resort is almost finished and the designers can take it from here. I wish you much success in your endeavors, and if you by some miracle decide you want to be a proper father to our child, send me an email and we'll make arrangements then."

"I would prefer a face-to-face meeting."

"I wouldn't." A personal encounter would take away her advantage and possibly strip of her strength.

Not waiting for Tarek's response, Kira rushed out of the room and retired to her quarters. She had no expectations when it came to Tarek Azzmar. She also didn't expect the tears streaming down her face would end anytime soon. She could foolishly hope that he might come around, or she could move on with her life without him.

Her hand automatically came to rest protectively on her belly. Sadly she would always have a little reminder of him, no matter what the future held.

"May we come in?"

Kira unpacked the last of her clothes before turning to discover sisters-in-law, Madison and Piper Mehdi, standing in the bedroom doorway. "You two girls are always welcome so feel free to come in."

"Girls" being the operative word in that instance considering the two closed the door and practically bounced onto the bed. "Thank you, Kira," Piper said, her palms resting atop of her T-shirt covered pregnant belly. "We had to have a break from toddler central. The kids are absolutely wild today. Sam's on a sugar high, thanks to his grandmother giving him two cookies."

"Mine are more than wild," Madison said as she tightened her blond ponytail. "I've never liked the term 'double trouble' when referring to twins, but that describes the way they've been acting since they awoke at dawn."

Kira cleared away the folded clothes from the club chair and set them on the bureau before claiming a seat. "How is the new governess handling everything since I hired her?"

Piper tucked one bent leg beneath her and twisted her elaborate wedding rings round and round on her finger. "I'm worried she might quit today."

Madison fell back on the bed and stared at the ceiling. "I'm worried Zain is going to start hounding me to have another baby. I just got the twins fully potty-trained."

Piper playfully slapped her arm. "You know you want another one. Or at least you like the procreation process."

"Yes I do," Madison said with a smile. "I can't imagine what would've happened if Zain hadn't stopped me from leaving and I had to raise the babies on my own."

That struck a deep chord in Kira. She really had no place to go except for Canada and that could prove to be a disaster. "Luckily you didn't have to face that."

Madison's grin deepened. "True, and he got two babies for the price of one."

"Adan did let me leave," Piper began, "but I have to give him credit for coming after me in the States with his heart in his hands once he learned he couldn't live without me."

She certainly couldn't count on Tarek returning to profess his undying love. "And now he has a mother for his son and a new baby on the way. Both of you have done very well for yourselves in the procreation department."

Madison popped up like a jack-in-the box. "Since we're on that subject, did you do any procreating with Tarek Azzmar on your trip?"

If she didn't know better, she'd think both Madison and Piper were privy to her pregnancy. "I went on the trip to work, not procreate." That had happened before the trip.

After leaving the bed to press her palms against her lower back, Piper sent Kira a skeptical look. "Are you sure about that? I would swear you're practically glowing, or maybe that's a blush."

Kira automatically touched her flaming cheeks. "It's a little warm in here."

"Speaking of Tarek, go get the picture, Piper."

"It's not finished yet," Piper said.

Pointing toward the door, Madison told her, "It's finished enough. Now go fetch it from the hall."

Feigning a pout, Piper retreated out the door, muttering something about not being a dog. She returned a few moments later and held up a portrait of a thirty-something man. "As the official palace artist, my mother-in-law commissioned me to do this for her private collection. She gave me a photo of King Aadil in the prime of his life. Apparently it's her favorite and I can certainly see why. He was one good-looking king."

Kira could barely contain her shock over how much Tarek looked like him. Then again, she could be imagining things because she missed him so much. "That's absolutely some of your best work to date, Piper. She's going to love it."

"Don't you think he looks like Tarek?" Madison said, echoing Kira's thoughts.

Kira shrugged. "They're both of Middle Eastern descent and both nice-looking men. Aside from that, I'm not seeing it." However, she was telling one whopper of a lie.

"I think the resemblance is uncanny," Piper said. "Maybe he's Aadil's secret son."

Kira almost choked on air. "That is exactly how nasty rumors get started."

"True," Madison replied. "And when that happens, it's my job as the palace press secretary to explain them away, so stop it right now, Piper."

Piper rested the photo against the wall and reclaimed a spot on the edge of the mattress. "Seriously, Kira, we both noticed you and Tarek flirting months ago. Are you sure nothing happened between the two of you in Cyprus?"

Madison came to her knees and looked like a pooch begging for a bone. "Come on. We're all friends. Give us the dirty details."

For reasons that defied logic, tears began to well in Kira's eyes. "I'm sorry," she muttered. "It's just that…" She sniffed and decided to stop talking now before she started sobbing.

Piper scowled. "If that jerk did something to hurt you, I'm going to have Adan beat him up."

"I'll sick Zain on him, too," Madison added. "Not that I don't think Adan can hold his own, but Tarek is a really big hunk of a guy."

Piper's scowl melted into a grin over the faux pas. "You mean hulk of a guy."

"Both," Madison said.

That only made Kira want to cry more. "Since the two of you will probably find out sooner or later, Tarek and I did have a relationship for a while. But I'd appreciate it if you wouldn't say anything to the brothers. If they know I was fraternizing with a palace guest, I might be looking for a job. As it is, I'm worried they already suspect something's been going on."

Madison waved a hand in dismissal. "Don't worry about that, Kira. Men are obtuse when it comes to picking up signals unless it involves their personal radar."

Piper nodded in agreement. "And sometimes not even then. I practically had to tattoo my feelings to Adan's forehead before he figured it out."

An option Kira might entertain, if she ever saw Tarek again. "Just so you know, it's over between us. As nice as it was, it simply wasn't meant to be. He's not the kind of man who's searching for a serious re-lationship."

A shrill singsong sound had Madison pulling a cell phone out of her pocket and scanning a text. "It's the poor governess. She wants to know if it's okay if the kids have more cookies."

"Heck no," Piper said as she pushed off the bed. "We better get back to the nursery and run interference. It's time for Sam's nap anyway."

"I could use a nap," Madison said as she followed suit. "But knowing my little munchkins, that's not going to happen."

They both doled out hugs to Kira before heading out the door. "Kira, if you need to talk, you know where to find us," Piper began as she paused with her hand on the knob, "but sometimes life turns on a dime, so don't give up on Tarek yet."

Kira saw no good reason not to give up on him. She did see a valid reason to call him—the portrait. No, that wouldn't be wise. Besides, this was Tarek's pater-nity battle to undertake. As it was, she had enough on her hands with her own paternity issues. She had no idea how she would resolve the, but she did know she was weeks away—if not months—from successfully mending another broken heart.

For the past two weeks, the transition had come slowly but surely, and painfully.

Tarek had tried unsuccessfully to forget about Kira. How could he when everything reminded him of her? Every detail at the resort, every dawn, every sunset.

He had gone to bed alone, and awakened reaching for a woman whom he missed terribly, only to find an empty space where she had been.

Now he waited outside Elena Battelli's private quarters, seeking answers he required to move away from his past, as Kira had urged him to do. She had forced him to open old wounds, left him to bleed alone, and assess the direction his life had taken. He had not liked what he had discovered.

Tarek rapped twice on the mahogany door and waited for the woman to answer his summons, which she did immediately.

"Come in, Mr. Azzmar," she said with a sweeping gesture toward the small parlor. "Please have a seat."

Tarek chose the small blue sofa while Elena took the paisley chair across from him. "I appreciate you agreeing to meet me on such short notice," he began, "but I felt this could not wait a moment longer."

She studied him with keen eyes. "Kira told me you suspected Aadil was your biological father, so we will dispense with all pleasantries and get to the point. Was your mother's name Darcia?"

Hearing the name had a startling effect on him. "Yes, it was."

"Then I have something I must show you."

She pushed out of the chair, disappeared into another room and returned a few moments later holding a yellowed piece of paper and a brown portfolio beneath her arm. "She sent this to Aadil. Read it."

He managed to take the offered letter, unfolded it and began to scan the text written in Arabic. He immediately recognized his mother's script from cards she had given him during his childhood. The content itself verified the covert relationship and contained a demand that the king never contact her again.

He turned his attention from the missive to Elena who had reclaimed the chair. "There is no mention of my mother's pregnancy or anything about me."

"It's clear in the letter Darcia believed they could not be together permanently since he was promised to another. She perhaps saw no need to inform Aadil."

The fury he had felt for so many years returned. "Then I am no closer to learning if he was, in fact, my father."

"Not necessarily," she said. "One evening many years ago, Aadil told me that your mother was the love of his life and he intended to give up the throne for her. When he returned to Morocco, she had moved away from her parents' home and into your father's house. He managed to find her and when he discovered she was pregnant, he confronted her about the baby's parentage. She denied you were his child and asked him to leave. He always believed otherwise, but he never bothered her again and went on to assume his duties as king."

"Suspicion does not equal fact."

"But this does." She opened the portfolio resting in her lap, withdrew what appeared to be newspaper clippings and handed them to Tarek. "He followed every step of your rise to fame and fortune as if he were searching for proof."

Tarek flipped through the photos and articles featuring him then returned them to Elena. "This is not proof of anything other than a man obsessing over the son born to a woman he could not have."

Elena pulled one last piece of paper from the folder and offered it to him. "Yet this is irrefutable."

A few seconds passed before Tarek understood what he was reading—a DNA report containing his and the former king's name. Most important, the test concluded that the results were 99.9999 percent positive he was the offspring of the former king. Still, he had more questions before he would let himself believe. "How did he obtain my DNA?"

Elena lifted her frail shoulders. "He was a very powerful man with many connections. I actually did find a written account from a private investigator outlining an unnamed person he was following in Morocco and that he gathered a paper cup the subject discarded in a trash bin. I assume that subject was you."

The information was almost too much to digest. "Then I suppose my mother had been truthful to her husband."

"My guess would be that he rescued Darcia from the shame of giving birth to a child out of wedlock. That was looked upon unfavorably forty years ago. I also think Aadil never sought you out to save you from shame as well."

"I believe now that was most likely the case." And as he considered that he would never know his biological father, a certain sadness replaced the ever-present anger.

When Tarek offered Elena the paper, she waved it

away. "You've waited many years for confirmation, so you should keep it."

"Thank you. Now that I have the information, I will have to consider what I should do with it in regard to my recently discovered brothers."

Elena presented a kindly smile. "Of course you should tell them."

His intent all along, yet everything had changed, including his attitude toward them. "I am not certain they will forgive my deceit."

"Rafiq might be hesitant to welcome you into the fold, but Zain and Adan should have no issues with accepting you into the family. And if you'll notice the date on the report, Aadil received it the week before his death. I believe he sensed he didn't have much longer on this earth, and this was the last bit of unfinished business. If he would have known sooner, he would have shown you the same care and concern as he did for his other sons."

"I would like to believe that to be true."

"I would like to believe you have learned something from this journey in regard to your own unborn child."

He should not be surprised Kira had confided in her. "How long have you known about the pregnancy?"

"Since the day Kira found out. She needed a shoulder to lean on and a listening ear. Of course, I encouraged her to tell you, though I was surprised she waited so long to do so."

He could not fault her for that. "I am still uncertain how to proceed. In many ways I feel as though I am not worthy to be a father."

Elena leaned over and laid her hand on his. "It's true that any man can procreate, but it takes a special man to take on fatherhood. You will make many mistakes but the rewards are very great. And would you subject your child to what you have endured, spending a lifetime wondering about the man responsible for his or her birth?"

The woman possessed uncanny wisdom. "No, I would not."

She leaned back, looking quite satisfied. "Excellent. Now what are you going to do about your child's mother?"

He saw no easy answer to that. "I will support her in every way possible."

"Every way?"

"In all ways that she will allow."

"Do you love her, Tarek?"

He'd once thought himself incapable of that emotion. He had recently learned that was false. "It matters not how I feel."

He still could not form the word for fear it would make him too vulnerable. "I proposed marriage and she declined."

"Did you profess your love then?"

"I did not."

Elena muttered several Italian oaths, complete with hand gestures. "No wonder she didn't accept. I ask again, do you love her?"

He prepared to open himself up to the truth. "I have admittedly been miserable. I long for the day when I might see her again and finally express my true feelings for her, yet I worry that might never come to pass."

Elena scowled. "Poppycock. I will never understand why men are so stubborn that they cannot see what is right in front of their nose. You are in love with her and Kira loves you. She wants nothing more than to be by your side from this point forward. Would you deny her that? Would you deny your own child?"

No, he would not. Yet a serious problem still existed. "Before she left Cyprus, she also refused my offer of a meeting to discuss our child. She instructed me to send an email."

"Well, she deserves the opportunity to throw you out in person, or possibly take you back."

He longed for the latter but braced himself for the former. "I am at a loss as to how to accomplish that."

Elena chuckled. "Oh my, have you come to the right place. I happen to have some experience with playing Cupid."

He would welcome any assistance. "Do you have a plan in mind?"

"It would involve a bit of creativity and borderline deception."

He was growing somewhat concerned. "Deception has created our conflict."

She laid a dramatic hand below her neck. "This is necessary to achieve our goal. Kira will understand once she sees what she will gain."

"Then I will trust you on this."

Elena's expression turned somber. "First, I must

know you are ready to pursue a permanent relationship with her. If not, then we will not proceed."

"I am more than ready." Words he never thought he would say.

"Good. Now we will go over the details."

Something suddenly occurred to him. "Should I inform the Mehdi sons of my identity first?"

"Leave them to me."

Having Elena run interference would be to his benefit, though under normal circumstances, he would not allow someone else to fight his battles. "If you believe that would be best, I will agree."

"It would be best." Elena leaned forward, lowered her voice and said, "This is what we will do...."

"Are you busy?"

Seated at her office desk, Kira didn't bother to look up from the computer as she said, "Never too busy for you, Elena. What do you need?"

Elena pulled up a chair next to hers. "I was curious about your doctor's appointment."

She inputted the last budget item then shut down the program before turning her office chair toward her. "Maysa said everything is great. The baby's heartbeat is strong and next month I'll have my first ultrasound. I can find out the gender if I want to, but I'm not sure about that yet." She was sure about the disappointment over Tarek not sharing those moments.

"Have you heard from the father?" Elena asked, as if she'd read Kira's mind.

Annoying disappointment came back to roost. "Not a word. But I never really expected it."

Elena took a quick look at her watch. "If Tarek came to you and expressed his undying love, would you consider taking him back?"

In a heartbeat. "I see no reason to ponder that since it's never going to happen."

"One never knows, *cara*," she said as she checked the time again.

"Do you have an appointment, Elena?"

"No, but you do." She pushed out of the chair and patted her silver hair. "You have a meeting with Rafiq."

Kira did a mental rundown of her schedule. "Since when?"

"Since now. He sent me here to summon you to his study."

Wonderful. She had too much to do and too little left of the day. "Do you know what this is about?"

"I have a few ideas, but I feel it's best not to speculate."

Kira stood and headed toward the door. "I hope this doesn't take too long."

Elena muttered something in Italian from behind her as they headed to the king's private study. Once there, she rapped on the door and heard Rafiq tell her to come in.

The second she entered, Kira felt as if she'd walked into an inquisition conducted by well-dressed royals. Rafiq sat behind the desk, looking handsome and regal, as usual. Zain and Adan stood behind him, arms folded across their chests like sentries. Then her gaze tracked to the right of the Mehdi sons, where another man positioned at the window caught her immediate attention. To most, he would appear to be any handsome, highly successful mogul, but she knew him as the father of her unborn baby.

"What is this about?" Kira asked as soon as she could form a coherent sentence.

"That's what I'd bloody like to know," Adan said.

"I would as well," Zain added. "My wife and I plan to have dinner in the village and have a night away from the twin follies."

Elena came to her side and laid a protective hand on Kira's shoulder. "If you would be patient, all will be revealed by Mr. Azzmar in short order."

As if on cue, Tarek stepped forward and cleared his throat. "I have asked you here today to reveal that I have not been completely truthful to any of you."

Rafiq sent him a hard look. "We are well aware that you and Kira have been involved in a tryst."

Kira exchanged a concerned look with Tarek before she said, "I promise we had no intention—"

"We didn't have to be rocket scientists to figure out, Kira," Adan interjected. "You both practically drool in each other's presence."

"The staff members have also entertained suspicions," Rafiq added. "Nothing is sacred in the palace."

Kira's cheeks heated like a furnace. "I don't know what to say except I'm very sorry."

Tarek took a step forward. "You cannot hold Kira accountable for my actions. And my personal relationship with her is only part of the reason why I called you here."

Zain shifted impatiently in the chair. "Then could you please clarify immediately?"

Tarek paced the room as if gathering his thoughts before facing the brothers to speak again. "Investing in Bajul is not my primary reason for being here. It never was. I arrived here seeking information and as of this morning, I have found it."

Kira held her breath as Tarek launched into his suspicions about his mother's involvement with the former king, his presumed father's revelation and his need to know his true parentage. He concluded by saying, "With Elena's aid, I now have the proof I have required for most of my adulthood. I am Aadil Mehdi's biological child, and your half brother."

The Mehdi sons sat for a time in stunned silence, until Rafiq regarded Elena. "Is this the truth?"

Elena squeezed Kira's shoulder before answering. "Yes, it is. There is no doubt that Tarek is your father's son. His relationship with Tarek's mother happened before he wed your mother, and he remained unaware he had another child for many years. He managed to confirm that fact shortly before his death."

"Bloody hell," Adan said. "The man did get around. Is there any chance there are more Mehdis primed to crawl out of the woodwork? The last time we had one of these little soirees I learned the woman I always thought of as my mother was actually my mother."

"Hush, my child," Elena told him. "Tarek has not finished speaking his mind."

Kira saw a hint of self-consciousness in his expression before he resumed his steel persona. "I do not expect any of you to readily accept this rather shocking turn of events, but I do hope I have your blessing on what I am about to tell you now."

He turned toward Kira and held out his hand. "If you would please join me."

She strode toward him in a fog, her head whirling with possibilities, and took his offered hand. As they stood there before the king's court, she feared her knees might not hold her.

"As you know," Tarek began, "Kira and I have grown very close—"

"I'm sure that is an understatement," Zain muttered, earning a quelling look from Elena. "I am only saying that you are a Mehdi, and with that comes a certain amount of virility and lack of control." That earned Adan's chuckle.

Surprisingly, Tarek smiled. "Regardless, I recognize you are all very protective of Kira, and I want to be clear on my commitment to her. She is everything a man could desire in a woman."

Kira practically gasped. "You want a commitment?"

"I definitely do. I did not realize this until you had left me."

"I want that, too, Tarek, but—"

"Enough with the moon-eyed declarations," Rafiq muttered. "Get on with it."

Tarek turned his focus back to the brothers. "In the absence of her father, I am asking you for permission to propose marriage to her."

While Kira stood frozen on the spot, the brothers nodded at each other before Rafiq rose from the chair. "If you will treat her with the respect she deserves, you have our blessing."

Tarek turned to Kira, a satisfied look on his face. "Kira Darzin, will you honor me by being my wife?"

How badly she wanted to say yes, but she couldn't in good conscience. Not yet. "No."

Ten

Tarek was somewhat stunned she was rebuffing him again, only this time in front of an audience. "You do not wish to be my wife?"

"I'm not saying I won't marry you. I'm saying my answer depends on your reasons for wanting to marry me."

His answer would require putting away his manly pride, he realized, when he glanced at the brothers who sat patiently awaiting his response, seemingly enjoying his predicament. "I vow to you that I will love you now and forevermore."

"You love me?" she asked, sheer wonder in her voice.

"I do."

Still, she did not seem quite satisfied. "And our baby?"

He sensed the sudden tension in the room. "I will love our child as I love you, and I will endeavor to be the best father possible."

Finally, she smiled. "Then my answer is a yes, I will marry you, Tarek Azzmar."

"You are with child, Kira?" Rafiq asked before Tarek could finally take Kira into his arms.

His future wife turned her attention to the king and frowned. "Yes, but we didn't plan that, either. Regardless, we're both very happy about it now."

"Cripes, we're going to have to expand the nursery," Adan groused.

Zain came to his feet. "Worse, we are going to have to replace Kira."

Elena stepped forward. "No need to worry about that. I will be in charge until we find a replacement...."

As the chaotic discourse continued, Tarek saw the opportunity to escape. He took Kira by the hand and said, "Come with me," As he led her to the door.

Before they could make a hasty exit, Zain called out, "Tarek, you will now be required to sit on the governing council."

Tarek raised his hand in acknowledgement and left out the door, closing it behind him. He led Kira down the corridor, and when they turned the corner, he seized the opportunity to kiss her thoroughly.

Once they parted, she looked at him with concern. "Are you absolutely sure about taking this step?"

More sure than he had ever been about any decision he had made at this juncture in his life. "I have not experienced such certainty for many years. Now, if you will join me upstairs, I have something I would like to show you."

She feigned a stunned look. "Oh my, Tarek. I realize the brothers seem to be fine with us, but do you think that's appropriate in the palace?"

He could not resist kissing her again. "That was not my intent, at least not presently. When we leave here later, I will give you an appropriate ravishing."

"I'm all for that."

They traveled to the second floor and paused at the door to the nursery, where the sounds of childish voices filtered into the hallway. "Let me guess," Kira said. "You've already set up a crib for our baby."

"I reserve that for our home," he said as he opened the door and searched for the little brown-haired, brown-eyed girl. He spotted her in the corner playing with a slew of stuffed animals and Zain Mehdi's twins under the watchful eye of a young governess. When he summoned Yasmin in Arabic, she looked up and favored him with a bright smile.

"Poppy!" she shouted as she ran toward him, her curls bouncing in time with her gait.

Tarek lifted her into his arms and turned to Kira. "This is Yasmin. Yasmin, this is Kira."

The absolute awe on Kira's face was worth all the gold in the hemisphere. "I am very pleased to meet you, Yasmin."

The little girl reached out and touched Kira's cheek. "You are very pretty."

"So are you, sweetheart. And you speak very good English."

Yasmin shrugged and pointed at Tarek. "He taught me. May I play now, Poppy?"

Tarek set her on her feet and knelt on her level. "You may, as soon as I give you a gift."

Yasmin rocked back and forth on her heels with barely-contained excitement. "Is it another puppy?"

"No, yet I believe you will like it." He withdrew one of the two black velvet boxes from his pocket. "Open this for me."

After Yasmin complied, her eyes filled with surprise when she saw the tiny silver band. "Is this mine?"

"Yes, it is." Tarek slipped the ring from the holder and held it up. "If you agree to be my daughter."

She pretended to pout. "I am your daughter, silly Poppy."

He pocketed the empty box and slid the band on her right ring finger. "Yes, and this makes it official."

She threw her arms around his neck and kissed his cheek. "I am going to show Cala and Joseph my ring now."

When she started away, he gently clasped her arm to halt her progress, took her by the shoulders and turned her around. "What do you say to Kira?"

"It is nice to meet you," she replied, followed by an exaggerated curtsy, then rushed back to her playmates.

Tarek escorted Kira back into the corridor and kissed her again. "I have arranged for some private time for us for a few hours. How do you suggest we spend that time?"

She stroked his jaw. "I can think of several pleasant things, but first I have to tell you that you giving Yasmin that ring meant so much to her, and me."

A long overdue gesture, in his opinion. "While we were apart, I arranged to adopt Yasmin so it will truly be official. However, I have put the process on hold since I would like to have you listed as her mother. I realize that is much to ask of you—"

She pressed a fingertip against his lips. "I would be honored to assume that responsibility, as long as Yasmin agrees."

"She will eventually, though it could require another mutt."

"I would hope loving her like my own would be enough to convince her to love me back."

He could not imagine any living being not loving an extraordinary woman such as Kira. "I am certain it will be, and we will tell her about the marriage very soon. Since meeting you, I have learned that being a good parent does not require blood ties. It involves caring and commitment and yes, making errors in judgment at times. I learned that long ago from my father, yet I allowed myself to forget those lessons."

She gently touched his cheek. "Do you think you can forgive your biological father for never acknowledging you?"

Before falling under Kira's positive influence, Tarek's answer would have been a definitive "No." "There is nothing to forgive. My mother gave him no choice in the matter. Unfortunately, when he finally made the effort to confirm that I was his son, it was too late. I do regret that."

She embraced him briefly and smiled. "Look at it

this way. You've gained an entire family. A somewhat eccentric family, but a loving family all the same."

"Yes, I have."

Her eyes suddenly went wide. "Oh no, I have to tell my parents about us and the baby before someone else does. I'm going to call them now but I left my cell phone in the office."

When Kira started away, Tarek clasped her hand to stop her. Apparently all the women in his life were bent on deserting him today. "Before you do that, I have a gift for you."

He withdrew the second box, opened it, and removed the second gift. "This is for you to make our engagement official."

Kira stared at the three-carat ruby and diamond ring, her eyes welling with tears. "It's beautiful, Tarek, but it's too much for a common girl like me."

He lifted her chin and kissed her cheek. "There is nothing common about you, Kira. You are an amazing woman deserving of all the best life has to offer."

She sent him a shaky smile. "I already have that in you."

After giving her one last kiss, he slipped the ring on her left hand, returned the box to his pocket, removed his own phone from his jacket and offered it to her. "You may call your parents now, and my wish is they will approve of our union."

"They will approve. Eventually." Kira took the cell and keyed in the number, a nervous look in her eyes. "Hi, Mama. I have something to tell you. I'm getting married."

* * *

"Now that your wedding day has arrived, dear daughter, I have something to give you."

After a final adjustment of the gold and diamond leaf headband securing the cathedral-length veil, Kira turned from the mirror to face Chandra Allain Darzin—the best mother anyone could ever want or need. She looked positively radiant and remarkably young in the cream-colored chiffon gown. "Let me guess. You're going to give me sage advice on how to keep my husband happy."

"Actually, I'm going to give you this." Chandra leaned over and withdrew a white box from her gold clutch, then opened it to reveal a dainty pearl bracelet with a small diamond heart-shaped pendant dangling from it.

"That's so beautiful, Mama. Was it grandmother's?"

"No. It's a gift from someone quite special."

Kira couldn't imagine who that might be. "Another relative?"

"The woman who blessed us with you. Your birth mother."

Tremors of shock ran through Kira, causing her hands to shake as she lifted the bracelet from the box to inspect it. "When did she give this to you?"

"Your eighteenth birthday. She sent it in the mail, along with a request not to open the box until your wedding day. This came with it." Her mother took out a folded piece of paper from her purse and handed it to her.

Since she didn't quite trust her own voice, Kira read the words in silence.

Dear Baby Girl,
This special bracelet belonged to my great-grandmother. I wore it on my wedding day and I felt the need to pass it on to you since it has brought me luck in my marriage.
I feel you should know that when you were born, I was barely a child myself and ill-equipped to care for a baby. As hard as it was to give you up, I knew the Darzins were good people and could give my child the life she deserved. I realize this simple gesture will never make up for my decision to let you go, but it's the best way I know how to show you that you have always been in my heart, if not in my arms, and will never be forgotten.
With love and wishing you much luck,
Janice

In that moment, any latent resentment Kira had directed toward her birth mother slipped away as her mother clasped the bracelet around her wrist. Any questions about whether the young woman responsible for her life cared at all, dissipated. The tears sliding down her cheeks were part relief, part sadness and in a large part, joy.

She shook off her melancholy and drew her mother—her real mother—into an embrace. "Thank you, Mama."

Chandra replaced the box with a handkerchief that

she used to swipe at her eyes. "You don't have to thank me, sweetheart. I had nothing to do with this."

"Maybe, but you had everything to do with who I am today. Because of you and Dad, I've learned the importance of forgiveness and the value of love."

Her mother sniffed then returned the hanky to her bag. "You have always been the absolute light of our lives, Kira. And you are such a beautiful bride. Now let's go find your father before he finds your young man and threatens him again."

After sharing in a laugh through the last of the tears, Kira and her mother walked arm-in-arm where she discovered her dad waiting in the vestibule, looking as if he might faint. When she heard the musical cue, she kissed her mother temporarily goodbye, then prepared to walk into her future with the man she adored and loved.

To the melodic strains of Bach's *Ave Maria,* Kira strolled down the aisle clinging tightly to her father's arm. She homed in on her mother seated in the first row, still dabbing at her eyes with the handkerchief. She then glanced at her papa and discovered he was looking rather misty, too. Sabir Darzin didn't cry, and at this rate she'd be blubbering before she reached the man standing at the front of the packed grand ballroom with the gleaming white marble floors. A gorgeous man wearing an immaculately tailored black silk tuxedo, a red rose pinned to his lapel and a welcoming smile on his face.

She barely noticed Madison and Piper, dressed in gold shimmering gowns, standing to his right, or their tuxedo-bedecked husbands, Zain and Adan, standing to his left. She did notice Yasmin walking ahead, tossing rose petals with abandon, and that Rafiq wore a white sash with the Mehdi family coat of arms embossed in gold as he waited to preside over the ceremony.

Before she stepped up on the temporary dais decorated with white roses, her dad paused, kissed her cheek and whispered, "I wish you luck, my precious daughter, and should this man not treat you well, I am not so old that I cannot take him on."

Kira returned his smile. "I promise that won't be necessary, Daddy, but thank you for the offer to defend my honor."

After he let her go, Kira held up the flowing floor-length white satin gown with the empire waist that somewhat concealed her growing abdomen and handed off her red-rose bouquet to Madison. She frankly didn't care what anyone thought about her pregnant-bride status. She only cared about her future husband, who held out his hand to her.

She came to Tarek's side and listened intently to Rafiq as he delivered a message regarding the responsibilities required for a successful marriage. After he finished, he instructed the bride and groom to face each other to deliver their own personal vows.

At that moment, every word she'd planned to say flew out of her brain, so she opted to speak from the heart. "Tarek, you were a pleasant, albeit unexpected, surprise. I choose you to be my husband for your compassion, your capacity for great love and your commitment to our children, present and future. The yacht doesn't hurt, either." After the spattering of laughter died down, she finished by saying, "I love you with all my heart, and always will."

Tarek looked down for a moment, and when he returned his gaze to hers, Kira saw unmistakable emotion reflecting from his eyes. He declared his love in Arabic, spoke his feelings about her in French, then concluded in English. "I stand before these witnesses and my family to vow that you will not want for anything during our life together. I look forward to waking with you by my side every morning, retiring with you each night and spending my days in pursuit of your happiness, for if you are truly happy, then so am I. I also vow to be actively involved in midnight feedings and diaper-changing, as ordained by my brother Adan."

Another bout of chuckles ensued, yet Tarek's expression grew serious. "What you have taught me has more value than any fortune. I love you, *rohi*."

My soul...

For Kira, that said it all.

"With the power vested in me as the king of the sovereign country of Bajul, I respectfully pronounce you husband and wife. And since you are clearly impatient to do so, you may now kiss your bride, Tarek."

Per Rafiq's final directive, Tarek put his arms around Kira and gave her a gentle, heartfelt kiss. Madison returned the bouquet to Kira before they left the dais and headed down the aisle to applause and well-wishes.

When they reached the hallway, Tarek guided Kira

into his private study and closed the door. He came back to her and drew her into a close embrace.

"Shall we begin the honeymoon now?"

Kira playfully slapped at his arm with the flowers. "We have to attend the reception first."

He nuzzled her neck. "They will not miss us as long as there is food."

And there would be a lot of food. Kira had been actively involved in planning the ceremony for the past month, when she hadn't been hanging out in bed with her fiancé. "Patience, my dear husband. We have plenty of time for that. After all, you'll have me all to yourself for three weeks on your yacht."

He grinned like the sexy devil he could be. "And we can be very daring."

"As long as no one sees my enlarging stomach."

He touched the place that housed their child with such sweet reverence, Kira almost cried. "This is for my eyes only. And you are still beautiful."

With Tarek, she sincerely felt beautiful. "Well, husband, now that we're married and we've moved Yasmin here, guess there's only one thing left to do, aside from the honeymoon."

He sent her a quizzical look. "What would that be, wife?"

"Have a baby."

"I swear this baby is never going to get here!"

As he smoothed his palm over Kira's damp forehead, Tarek had never felt so helpless in his life. "Soon, *rohi*."

"Very soon," Maysa said from her perch at the end of the bed. "I need one more push, Kira."

Panic was reflected in his wife's eyes. "What if I can't do that?"

"You will," Tarek said as he slid his arms beneath her for support.

Kira's low moan shot straight to his soul, but his baby's cry shot straight to his heart. He glanced toward the sound to see Maysa lifting the child up and saying, "It's a girl!" As she placed the baby on Kira's chest, Tarek witnessed her motherly instincts immediately set in, touching him deeply.

"My sweet baby girl," she cooed while the nurse covered the baby in a blanket. She then sent Tarek a worried look. "Are you disappointed she's not a boy?"

He laid his palm on his daughter's tiny back, experiencing an abiding love he never expected to feel. "Not in the least. Boys create trouble wherever they go. I am proud to have two daughters."

Kira touched his cheek. "Two beautiful daughters. I can't wait for Yasmin to see her as soon as she's finished with her lessons."

"She will be quite pleased we have given her a sister." As he was quite pleased that he had given her his name, and an outstanding mother.

Ignoring the flurry of activity and sounds coming from the hospital halls, they remained that way for a while, bonding as a family, marveling over the new life they had made. Tarek experienced an abiding love, an emotion he'd never expected to feel so deeply until he had allowed this woman into his heart, and his adopted daughter into his home, though he had once been reluctant to admit it to himself. That was no longer the case.

"We're going to take the baby now to weigh her and examine her," Maysa said, interrupting the emotional interlude. "We won't be gone long."

Kira seemed hesitant to let her go. "Hurry back," she said after she relinquished their child to the nurse.

Tarek pulled a chair up to the bedside and took his beloved wife's hand. "You were braver than most men."

Kira released a cynical laugh. "I turned into a sniveling, whiny wimp."

"Understandable since you were in pain."

"Yes, that was some pain. But now that it's over, what are we going to call her?" she asked.

A debate that had been ongoing for some time. "I believe we should go with what you prefer. Using our mothers' middle names."

Kira looked as if he had handed her the key to the universe. "Then Laila Anne Azzmar it is, although Yasmin will insist on calling her Annie."

"I have no issue with that."

Either name would suit her well. This life suited him well. He had come a long way as the son of two commoners who had learned he was the son of a king. He had built a fortune, achieved resounding success, yet nothing could compare to his greatest accomplishment—learning to love. From this point forward, he was prepared to continue this greatest of adventures with the treasured woman whom he loved with all that he was, or would be.

And as the nurse returned their beloved child and placed her in his arms, Tarek Azzmar, billionaire mogul, knew what it meant to be truly blessed.

Epilogue

Kira had discovered a long time ago that Mehdi family gatherings were quite an adventure, though before she had been on the outside looking in. Before there weren't quite as many Mehdis, either. As she sat at a table beneath a copse of olive trees on the palace grounds, holding her sleeping six-week-old against her breasts, she took a quick look around and smiled at the scene. Yasmin and Cala were attempting to climb a brick retaining wall, ignoring the fact they were wearing party dresses. Joseph stood nearby, egging them on and calling them babies when they couldn't quite achieve their goal.

In the distance, Adan held his toddler son, Sam, while his wife, Piper, cradled their three-month-old, Brandon. And standing beside them, the formerly-widowed

Mehdi military cousin, Sheikh Rayad Rostam, had his hands full with yet another newborn son who carried his father's name, while his new wife, Sunny, looking exhausted, rested her head on his shoulder. Rafiq entered the picture, chasing after young Prince Ahmed, who'd just learned to walk, while Maysa trailed behind him, laughing. But Kira had yet to locate Tarek, who had disappeared twenty minutes ago.

Elena, Zain and Madison soon arrived with a tray of refreshments that they placed on the lengthy table nearby. After shifting Laila to her shoulder, Kira came to her feet and joined the group for the festivities.

She then felt two strong arms come around her from behind and a kiss on her neck. Missing husband found. "Where have you been?" she asked him when he moved to her side.

He took the baby from her grasp and held her against his broad shoulder. "I had to finalize the purchase on a new yacht."

"We have a perfectly good yacht."

He gently kissed Laila's cheek, causing Kira's heart to take a little tumble in her chest. "This one is child-proofed and has more cabins. We need extra room to house the children. I predict we will have a son very soon."

"I'll get right on that."

He had the gall to grin. "We can begin tonight."

"We can pretend tonight. I'd like to wait until this little one is out of diapers before we make another one."

"I suppose I can agree to that, as long as we do quite a bit of pretending."

She saw no problem with that. "When can I see the new yacht?"

"The *Kira* should be delivered to the port in Oman in ten days."

The man was still full of surprises. "You named a boat after me?"

"Of course. A beautiful watercraft should always carry the name of a beautiful woman."

She could so kiss him for that, and she did.

"Gather round, adults and many small creatures," Adan called out. "It is time to toast our good fortune."

Knowing the youngest prince, Kira expected anything to come from his mouth. She hooked her arm through her husband's and claimed a place at the table next to Elena, who smiled and patted Kira's back. For months, she had thanked the former governess, matchmaker and mentor for her role in bringing Tarek to his senses, though Elena had claimed every time she had only been doing her job.

As Adan held up his glass, everyone followed suit. "To children, the future of Bajul. And should anyone else in attendance be pregnant, please notify us immediately so that we might add another wing to the palace, or respectfully find another place to live."

As soon as the laughter died down, Adan continued. "And now, in the words of my dear Italian mother, *la Famiglia!*"

"To family!" everyone repeated in unison.

Kira looked around at the people surrounding her and felt completely immersed in love. This was an extension of her family. This was the place she wanted to remain. And when spring rolled around, her parents would be relocating to Bajul, her father's homeland, making Kira's world complete.

She then gave her attention to her children and realized the best things came in small packages. She'd learned forgiveness was always attainable in the presence of true love, and fate handed you gifts when least expected.

The greatest gift slid his hand into hers and looked as if she were the most important person on the planet. Her handsome husband. The man of her dreams, who possessed her heart. He might be the consummate billionaire mogul, but she could think of a billion reasons why he was the consummate man and father.

For Kira Darzin Azzmar, life didn't get any better than this.

* * * * *

If you loved this book from
Kristi Gold, pick up her other sheikh stories!

THE RETURN OF THE SHEIKH
ONE NIGHT WITH THE SHEIKH
THE SHEIKH'S SON

Available now from Harlequin Desire!

If you're on Twitter, tell us what you think of
Harlequin Desire! #harlequindesire

#2383 THE BILLIONAIRE'S DADDY TEST
Moonlight Beach Bachelors • by Charlene Sands
Mia D'Angelo will not turn over her niece to the baby's unsuspecting father until she knows the reclusive billionaire is daddy material. But when Adam Chase uncovers her ruse, he's ready to make his own very personal demands...

#2384 SEDUCED BY THE SPARE HEIR
Dynasties: The Montoros • by Andrea Laurence
When black-sheep Prince Gabriel unexpectedly finds himself in line to the throne, he turns to Serafia Espina to revamp his image. But when they go from friends to lovers, a family secret resurfaces, threatening everything they've begun.

#2385 PREGNANT BY THE COWBOY CEO
Diamonds in the Rough • by Catherine Mann
Amie McNair spent one impulsive night with the McNair empire's new CEO, Preston Armstrong. Now she's pregnant! Can she keep her secret when they must travel—in close quarters—on a two-week cross-country business trip?

#2386 LONE STAR BABY BOMBSHELL • by Lauren Canan
It isn't until *after* their one-night stand that Kelly realizes Jace isn't just a handsome cowboy—he's an award-winning actor and a notorious playboy. Now that he's back in town, how will she tell him he's a father?

#2387 CLAIMING HIS SECRET SON
The Billionaires of Black Castle • by Olivia Gates
Billionaire Richard Graves escaped from his mercenary past years ago, but he still wants his enemy's widow for himself. When their lives collide again, can he let go of old wounds despite the secret she's been keeping?

#2388 A ROYAL AMNESIA SCANDAL • by Jules Bennett
After her royal boss's accident, assistant Kate Barton must pretend to be the fiancée he doesn't remember leaving. But soon her romantic role becomes all too real. How will she explain her pregnancy when his memory returns?

REQUEST YOUR FREE BOOKS!

2 FREE NOVELS PLUS 2 FREE GIFTS!

H HARLEQUIN®

Desire

ALWAYS POWERFUL, PASSIONATE AND PROVOCATIVE

YES! Please send me 2 FREE Harlequin® Desire novels and my 2 FREE gifts (gifts are worth about $10). After receiving them, if I don't wish to receive any more books, I can return the shipping statement marked "cancel." If I don't cancel, I will receive 6 brand-new novels every month and be billed just $4.55 per book in the U.S. or $5.24 per book in Canada. That's a savings of at least 13% off the cover price! It's quite a bargain! Shipping and handling is just 50¢ per book in the U.S. and 75¢ per book in Canada.* I understand that accepting the 2 free books and gifts places me under no obligation to buy anything. I can always return a shipment and cancel at any time. Even if I never buy another book, the two free books and gifts are mine to keep forever.

225/326 HDN GH2P

Name _____ (PLEASE PRINT)

Address _____ Apt. #

City _____ State/Prov. _____ Zip/Postal Code

Signature (if under 18, a parent or guardian must sign)

Mail to the **Reader Service:**

IN U.S.A.: P.O. Box 1867, Buffalo, NY 14240-1867
IN CANADA: P.O. Box 609, Fort Erie, Ontario L2A 5X3

Want to try two free books from another line?
Call 1-800-873-8635 or visit www.ReaderService.com.

* Terms and prices subject to change without notice. Prices do not include applicable taxes. Sales tax applicable in N.Y. Canadian residents will be charged applicable taxes. Offer not valid in Quebec. This offer is limited to one order per household. Not valid for current subscribers to Harlequin Desire books. All orders subject to credit approval. Credit or debit balances in a customer's account(s) may be offset by any other outstanding balance owed by or to the customer. Please allow 4 to 6 weeks for delivery. Offer available while quantities last.

Your Privacy—The Reader Service is committed to protecting your privacy. Our Privacy Policy is available online at www.ReaderService.com or upon request from the Reader Service.

We make a portion of our mailing list available to reputable third parties that offer products we believe may interest you. If you prefer that we not exchange your name with third parties, or if you wish to clarify or modify your communication preferences, please visit us at www.ReaderService.com/consumerschoice or write to us at Reader Service Preference Service, P.O. Box 9062, Buffalo, NY 14240-9062. Include your complete name and address.

HD15

SPECIAL EXCERPT FROM

Desire

When black sheep Prince Gabriel unexpectedly finds himself in line to the throne, he turns to Serafia Espina to revamp his image. Lessons on manners quickly turn to seduction—until family secrets tear them apart...

Read on for a sneak peek of
SEDUCED BY THE SPARE HEIR
by *Andrea Laurence*,
the latest in Harlequin® Desire's
DYNASTIES: THE MONTOROS series.

Gabriel took another step toward her, closing in on her personal space. With her back pressed against the oak armoire, she had no place to go. A part of her didn't really want to escape anyway. Not when he looked at her like that.

His dark green eyes pinned her in place, and her breath froze in her lungs. He wasn't just trying to flatter her. He did want her. It was very obvious. But it wasn't going to happen for an abundance of reasons that started with his being the future king and ended with his being a notorious playboy. Even dismissing everything in between, it was a bad idea. Serafia had no interest in kings or playboys.

"Well, I'll do my best to not annoy you, but I do so enjoy the flush across your cheeks and the sparkle in your dark eyes. My gaze is drawn to the rise and fall of your breasts as you breathe harder." He took another step closer. Now he could touch her if he chose. "If you don't want me to make you angry anymore, I could think of another way to get the same reaction that would be more...*pleasurable* for us both."

Serafia couldn't help the soft gasp that escaped her lips at his bold words. For a moment, she wanted to pull him hard against her. Every nerve in her body buzzed from his closeness. She felt the heat of his body radiating through the thin silk of her blouse. Her skin flushed and tightened in response.

One palm reached out and made contact with the polished oak at her back. He leaned in and his cologne teased at her nose with sandalwood and leather. The combination was intoxicating and dangerous. She could feel herself slipping into an abyss she had no business slipping into. She needed to stop this before it went too far. Serafia was first and foremost a professional.

"I'm not sleeping with you," she blurted out.

Gabriel's mouth dropped open in mock outrage. "Miss Espina, I'm shocked."

Serafia chuckled, the laughter her only release for everything building up inside her. She arched one eyebrow. "Shocked that I would be so blunt or shocked that I'm turning you down?"

He smiled and her knees softened beneath her.

"Shocked that you would think that was all I wanted from you."

Don't miss SEDUCED BY THE SPARE HEIR
by Andrea Laurence, part of the
DYNASTIES: THE MONTOROS series:

MINDING HER BOSS'S BUSINESS by Janice Maynard
CARRYING A KING'S CHILD by Katherine Garbera
SEDUCED BY THE SPARE HEIR by Andrea Laurence
THE PRINCESS AND THE PLAYER by Kat Cantrell
MAID FOR A MAGNATE by Jules Bennett
A ROYAL TEMPTATION by Charlene Sands

Only from Harlequin® Desire
www.Harlequin.com

JUST CAN'T GET ENOUGH?

Join our social communities
and talk to us online.

You will have access to the latest
news on upcoming titles and special
promotions, but most importantly,
you can talk to other fans about your
favorite Harlequin reads.

Harlequin.com/Community

f Facebook.com/HarlequinBooks

Twitter.com/HarlequinBooks

Pinterest.com/HarlequinBooks